AFTER SCHOOL ACTIVITIES

Dirk Hunter

Published by
DREAMSPINNER PRESS

5032 Capital Circle SW, Suite 2, PMB# 279, Tallahassee, FL 32305-7886 USA
http://www.dreamspinnerpress.com/

ISBN: 978-1-63216-541-1
Digital ISBN: 978-1-63216-542-8
Library of Congress Control Number: 2014920694
First Edition March 2015

Printed in the United States of America
∞
This paper meets the requirements of
ANSI/NISO Z39.48-1992 (Permanence of Paper).

CHAPTER ONE

SO FAR, today was shaping up to be a rather ordinary Tuesday. First period had barely begun, and I was already in the principal's office. Adam Anderson, my sworn enemy since kindergarten, sat in the chair next to me, arms crossed, staring sullenly at the floor. Me? I was grinning.

"All right, Mr. O'Connor," our principal, Theodore Hayes, said, looking at me from over steepled fingers. "Why don't you tell me what happened this time."

My grin widened, turned mischievous. "Theo. Darling, how many times do I have to tell you to call me Dylan?"

TEN MINUTES before the bell rang, the halls of Oak Lake High were swarming with kids. Even so, I couldn't help but overhear an unfortunately all too familiar sound: small-minded douchebaggery.

"Why, if it isn't a brand-new fairy boy for us to have a little fun with, right, boys?"

This, wafting from a less-traveled side hall where all the language classrooms were situated—empty this early, 'cause, you know, no language classes before third period. I couldn't help but sigh. Sure, I could have ignored it—and seriously, Mr. Hayes, I almost did—but honestly? I was a little hurt my nemesis was cheating on me with some unknown freshman. It stung.

So I took a stroll down the hall and found that—surprise surprise—dear old Adam here, along with two of his buddies, had cornered some poor kid I didn't recognize. Now, Oak Lake is a pretty small school; you get to know everyone, if not by name, then at least how they look. So I figured out pretty quickly that it was probably this kid's first week, else he might have thought twice before wandering alone down the language hall at all, much less with a bedazzled backpack. A My Little Pony backpack, to boot. Rookie mistake. I couldn't help but feel for the kid, you know?

"Come on, Adam." I said, interrupting a mess of giddy snickering, "didn't anyone tell you how uncool it is to date a freshman, no matter how much *fun* it is?"

The three bullies turned, with spectacular coordination—did you guys practice that, Adam? Spinning in sync?—but only Adam kept smiling. His buddies, at least, had the good grace to look ashamed. Now I won't name names, I don't do that, but let's just say one of them only passed math last semester 'cause I tutored him, and the other has an older brother who used to date my sister. But Adam, bless his heart, pressed on, not noticing his backup dancers were slowly inching away.

"Oh look. If it isn't King Queer, come to rescue one of his subjects," Adam said.

I sighed and shook my head. "Personally I would have gone with 'Queen Queer.' Not only for the whole, you know, gay thing, but also for the alliteration. Seems like a real missed opportunity." As I spoke, I stepped past Adam to talk to the new guy. "Hey, kid. Name's Dylan. Sorry about my man Adam here. He's got some issues with his masculinity." I brought my hand up to my mouth and whispered, loud enough for everyone to hear, "*Impotence*. You know how it is. Well, you probably don't. Anyway, welcome to Oak Lake High. I'd love to give you the tour, but I seem to be a bit preoccupied at the moment. Don't let that stop you, however, from running off and familiarizing yourself with any halls *other* than this one."

The new kid squeaked a thank-you and ran. Man, self-confidence, we should really teach that in school. Wouldn't you agree, Mr. Hayes?

"Alright, faggot," Adam growled, spinning me around and slamming me against the wall. "I guess it's just you and me now."

Now, at this point I started to get a little concerned. Adam here has done a lot of things to me in the past—good memories, every one—but he had never actually *grabbed* me like that before, you know? We mostly just traded clever insults back and forth. Well, mine were clever. I still couldn't believe you missed that "Queen Queer" gem, Adam. And by this point Adam's companions in crime had made themselves pretty scarce, so I couldn't even count on them to step in should things start to spiral downward. Honestly, I was a little concerned for my personal well-being.

Not that I was gonna allow that to stop me.

"Oh, Adam, you brute, you! You know how I like it when you take command like that. Such strength! Such power!"

Adam's cheeks colored. It was clear that I was getting to him. "We'll see how you like this power when it's punching you in the gut."

"Why, Mr. Cortez! Is that shining armor you're wearing? Tell me, do all English teachers have your sense of timing?"

"AND MR. Cortez said, 'Alright boys, break it up,' and Adam was like 'Not until my fist teaches this faggot a lesson, 'cause I'm a big strong man and I have to prove that every day. Arrrgghhhh.'"

"I didn't say that." Adam spoke up for the first time since being sent to Mr. Hayes's office.

"It was implied."

Adam opened his mouth to reply, but Mr. Hayes cut him off with a gesture. "Well, Mr. O'Connor—"

"Dylan."

"—that was very… thorough." He turned to Adam. "Mr. Anderson, you know we have zero tolerance for bullying and violence. I'm afraid I'm going to have to give you detention."

"But—"

"No buts, Mr. Anderson. You're dismissed." I stood up too, but Mr. Hayes wasn't quite finished with me. "And Mr. O'Connor, you could try provoking Mr. Anderson a little bit less. I'd give you detention also if I wasn't absolutely convinced it would be a huge mistake to keep you two in the same room. Next time, though, it's you who will be staying after school." Adam gave me a smug look. "Now go, both of you. There's no point in going to your first class. You'd disrupt more than it's worth. There's another ten minutes until second period, so I expect you to behave yourselves."

I SUPPOSE I should consider myself lucky—in a lot of schools, *I'd* have been the one getting the detention. They'd say I deserved what I got for "provoking" the other students, when it would really be because I was gay. At least when Mr. Hayes accused me of provoking Adam—and I suppose I did provoke Adam, a little—it was because of the insults, not my sexuality. Oak Lake, despite being such a small town, was actually pretty open-minded. Sure, it had its pricks, like Adam, but most of the homophobes were like Adam's friends from that morning. They'd pick on you for being gay, but not if they, like, knew you or anything. And as far as Adam went, he didn't really get any social points for picking on people. The other popular kids didn't really hold it against him either, but I'd take apathy to outright hatred any day. Baby steps, right?

As it was, Adam sat comfortably at the level of a duke, maybe an earl, in Oak Lake's popularity kingdom. For one thing, he was on the football team, which practically guaranteed you a place at the cool kids' table. For another, and perhaps most importantly, Adam was really, really hot. Not the hottest guy in school, of course. That honor was James P. Hogan's. All-star quarterback, perpetual prom king, with muscles in all the right places, each strand of brown hair falling perfectly to frame an exquisite face, eyes you could drown in even if you only accidentally saw them from the edge of your vision. James P. Hogan graced the halls of Oak Lake High with a perfect smile and a beautiful voice that could often be heard singing between classes, entrancing. He was the undisputed king of the school, but he was the most benevolent of rulers—no matter who you were, whether the most vapid of cheerleaders or the weirdest of nerds, he would happily stop to talk to you, laugh at your pathetic attempt at a joke, say how you were the best part of the drama club's production of *The Pirates of Penzance*, that you had the best singing voice he'd ever heard—which was hilarious: no one sang as well as James P. Hogan—and he'd touch your arm just so as he walked away, shooting a smile over his shoulder that could melt the heart of the straightest of men….

Sorry. I got a little carried away. Memory lane, and all that. Where was I? Oh, right. Adam.

Adam was probably the fourth hottest guy in Oak Lake, as such things are measured. Maybe the fifth, depending on how you feel about overly muscular men. Don't get me wrong, his body doesn't scream "steroids" or anything, but he's definitely closer to Captain America than Spiderman—James P. Hogan was a perfect Spiderman. Muscular without bulging. Lithe, that's the word. But I digress. Again.

Adam kept his blond hair short, and his eyes were as blue as the ocean—but too hard to get lost in. Not that you'd want to, of course. On those rare occasions when he smiled, and that smile wasn't filled with malice, anyway, even I could feel my pulse quicken. And I *hated* that guy.

Maybe that was why I was about to do something really, really dumb.

"Adam, wait up," I called, as we got out of Mr. Hayes's office. He stopped but didn't turn around.

"What?" His face was even sourer than usual.

"What's the matter with you today?"

He met my eyes for a split second, then looked away. "What the fuck are you talking about, faggot?"

"That, right there! That's the second time you've called me a faggot today. You usually put a lot more effort into this. You'll call me an anal excavator, or a rubber-wristed waste of space—you once called me Puck the Flying Fairy Fuck, which I'm *still* impressed with. Your insults used to be *Shakespearian*, man! But this? It's just lazy. It gives me nothing to work with. This hatred of ours is a two-way street, man. You have to give a little to get a little. I should have to struggle to think of a clever-enough comeback. I mean, I never will 'cause I'm amazing and you're an idiot—but I *should*. You usually only resort to dropping 'faggot' when you're too mad to come up with anything else. So I ask again, what's *wrong* with you today?"

"Seriously? You got me detention and you wonder if I'm too angry to play your stupid little games? I'm going to have to miss football practice, again. Coach is gonna be pissed, again…."

"You should have thought before you practiced your tackle on me this morning." I couldn't help it. Adam drew sarcastic comments out of me entirely against my will. But I regretted it pretty much immediately. Whatever he said, it was obvious Adam got just as much into our insult battles as I did. Something was definitely up, and my snide comments weren't gonna help anything. "Listen, if there's anything I can, I dunno, do…."

"Yeah," Adam snapped back at me. "You can go die in a fire."

Well. I don't know what I was expecting, exactly. Just then the bell rang. First period was over. I put Adam out of my mind and headed to class.

I MADE it to biology seconds after the bell rang. I still hadn't even been to my locker that morning, and it was on the opposite side of the school. Luckily, my two best friends had saved me a spot at our lab table in the back corner of the classroom. Waving apologetically to Mrs. Webster—a master of the disapproving stare, by the way, and today was no exception—I made my way over to my friends.

Kai leaned in as I sat down. "Let me guess. Another date with Adam and Mr. Hayes?"

I smiled. "Hooray Tuesdays."

"You provoked him again, didn't you?" Melanie whispered from the other side of Kai.

"Why is everyone accusing me of that today? I don't provoke. He's just an asshole." Mel gave me an "if you say so" look. "Anyway, thanks for saving me a seat."

"No problem. Mel wanted to give your seat to Kyle." He grinned at her.

Mel chuckled but didn't look his way. "I remember things differently," she said out of the corner of her mouth, pretending like she was listening to Mrs. Webster.

"Her exact words," he said, turning back to me, "were 'wouldn't it be hilarious if Dylan were trapped with half the cheer squad?' She sounded pretty sadistic too."

"Yeah, 'cause that doesn't sound like something you would say at all…."

I smiled, listening to my friends bicker. They'd been this way pretty much the instant Mel moved to Oak Lake in the fifth grade, arguing and teasing. Malachi and Melanie, Mal and Mel everyone called them. Except for me, of course. I'd shortened Malachi's name to Kai ever since the day I met him in kindergarten. "At least spell it C-H-I," he'd say every time I wrote his name. "Um, your name's not Chi," I'd say, and Mel would chime in that actually "chi" is spelled "qi," and she'd write out the Chinese character for it, as if that proved anything, and things would quickly devolve from there. It was our favorite argument.

Kai insisted he always knew I was gay, right from that very first day. He said it was 'cause I insisted on doing everything differently from everyone else, right down to which part of his name to call him. It was probably bullshit, of course—we didn't even know what gay *was* back then—but I kind of liked the idea; Kai had always known me better than anyone else, almost as well as I knew myself.

Come to think of it, Adam once said he knew I was gay in kindergarten too, 'cause I "pranced like a fairy," which was definitely bullshit. I rarely pranced.

"Hey, Dylan! You gonna sit there and take that?" Kai said, nudging me with his elbow.

"What?"

"Mel here is blaming your fight with Adam this morning on you redheads all having fiery tempers." Of course, making fun of my red hair was Kai's favorite pastime, not Mel's. She punched him in the side, her favorite way of saying "nope."

"Oh, sorry, I…" was dwelling on Adam, I realized. I know, I said I'd put him out of my mind, but it turned out to be easier said than done. It kept worrying away at me, and the more I thought about it, the more I became convinced something weird was going on. He'd never really seemed sullen before. Maybe I was just upset he'd called me a faggot twice. Not my favorite word, and ugh, I'd used it myself at least as many times today because of him. But I couldn't shake the feeling that there was something more going on and, worse, that it meant I might have to give the guy a break for a while. Which was *not* going to be fun. What else was I supposed to do during school if not bait the bully? Learn? Hardly.

But I couldn't tell Kai any of that. How do you explain to your best friend that you weren't listening to him 'cause you were thinking about your worst enemy? Plus, though Kai would never have admitted it, he tended to get more than a little jealous. He even got a little mad when I first started hanging out with Mel, and they had been friends first. If anyone should have been jealous in that situation, it should have been me.

"…I was trying to pay attention to Mrs. Webster." I finally landed on a good-enough excuse. "You know, there's a test on Friday."

Kai did not seem convinced. He gave me a look that promised I'd be hearing about this later. Even Mel turned to give me an incredulous stare, completely abandoning all pretense of paying attention. They knew something was up. I could feel my face flush. I felt kinda guilty about lying, but what was I supposed to tell them? I didn't really know what was going on myself. Just when it felt like I couldn't take their scrutiny for another second, the attendance sheet was passed to me, breaking the tension. I wrote all our names to sign us in.

"Oh come on, Dylan. At least spell it C-H-I."

Chapter Two

My vow to lay off Adam didn't even last the week. In my defense, he was totally asking for it. That Wednesday I noticed that new kid I had rescued across the lunchroom, spaghetti-filled tray in hand, making his way over to a table full of other little freshmen. I pointed him out to Mel and Kai—by this time, I had told them about my encounter Tuesday morning.

"It's nice to see he's made some friends," Mel said. "Being the new kid can be rough."

"Especially when Adam is throwing your welcome-to-the-school party," Kai quipped. "Speak of the devil…."

Not quite halfway to his destination, the new kid was stopped by a blockade of jocks, Adam in the lead. The kid looked to his friends for support, but they all stared back at him helplessly. No way were they going to draw the wrath of any junior, much less the most notorious bullies in the school. It was four on one, and I itched to even the odds.

"Don't get involved, Dylan. Mr. Hayes is gonna flip if you get sent in twice in a week. And you'll be the one getting detention this time. Let one of the teachers stop Adam," Mel said.

But neither of the teachers set to watch over the lunchroom seemed to notice. They were caught up in some discussion, oblivious to the plight of the underclassmen. As usual. Kai raised an eyebrow, obviously expecting me to step up and put Adam in his place.

"You're right, Mel," I mumbled dejectedly into my food. Kai nearly choked in surprise.

So I sat and watched, getting angrier and angrier with each malicious laugh that floated across the lunchroom. Mel kept trying to engage me in conversation but eventually quit, probably tired of me answering in grunts and monosyllables. Kai occasionally gave me sidelong looks, as if wondering who I was and what I'd done with the Dylan he knew. But he didn't say anything, which was probably for the best; the angrier I got the more likely it became that I'd accidentally snap at my best friend. It was probably only five minutes that I sat and watched, but it felt like an hour, and by the end of it, I was seething with rage.

See, I really felt for that kid.

In elementary school, I was often the victim of the older kids' desire to exert dominance, prove their masculinity, impress the equally small-minded ladies, or whatever their bullshit reason was. When Adam had joined in, I thought I would die. It was one thing to avoid kids a few grades above me, but Adam was around every minute of the day. I'd sit there, trying to hide my tears from everyone, even Kai, until one day I just snapped. I remembered it perfectly: I was in the third grade and we were outside for recess. The fifth graders' recess overlapped ours by about ten minutes, and every day those ten minutes were my personal hell. But this one day, I was cornered by the usual trio of bullies—shoving me, calling me a wimp, a fairy boy, a ginger freak—and I lost it. I turned to the shortest of the three—still taller than me, I might add—and let loose. Not with my fists, but with my *words*.

Years of pent-up aggression flowed out of me as I insulted his face, his intelligence, his family, anything that crossed my mind to use against this demon who'd tormented me for so long. I finally finished by saying that the only reason he liked to pick on me so much was because he just wanted to suck my tiny, third-grader dick. He turned bright red. It was awesome. And to my surprise, the other two started laughing. Hysterically. After a minute, so did the kid I'd just finished berating. From then on, it became less bullying and more a game: they'd insult me, I'd insult them, and the shoving stopped. And usually, I won. Best of all, I'd finally found a way to fight back against Adam without having to, you know, fight—Adam had always been much bigger than me.

Ever since then I'd made it my personal mission to get between a bully and his victim. I'd disarm them with wit, charm, and no small amount of humor. More often than not, they'd end up liking me in the end and give up the bullying, at least while I was around. So now, watching Adam bullying some poor little kid two years younger than us, a kid who had no chance of defending himself, was torture. The worst part was that I was doing it to spare the *bully's* feelings. What the fuck was wrong with me?

Right then, the new kid's lunch tray flew through the air, knocked out of his hands by Adam. From the table of freshmen, one of the kid's friends finally jumped up to go tell a teacher—things had gotten serious. I saw Adam step closer to the kid, using his height to menace, a mean grin on his face. Before I knew it, I was on my feet and halfway across the lunchroom.

Behind me, I heard Kai mutter, "Finally."

"You know what we do to little fag boys around here?" I'd gotten close enough hear what Adam was saying. The new kid looked like he was about to wet himself. Adam towered over him threateningly. Of course, Adam wasn't really gonna do anything. He'd never been one to actually attack a kid; his bullying stayed purely in the realm of the verbal. But while I knew this, the new kid definitely didn't.

"Oh, Adam, when will you learn?" Adam turned to me, malicious grin turning into a baleful frown. The new kid didn't need my prompting this time. As soon as his bully's back was turned, he ran. "Beating up on some poor kid will never make up for all the hugs Daddy never gave you."

It took me a minute to piece out what happened next. The first thing I noticed was that I was on the floor. The second, that everyone was yelling. Pain came third. I looked up at Adam, shock and rage playing across his face in equal parts.

"You punched me," I finally managed to say.

"OF ALL the stupid thing you've done, Mr. Anderson, this has got to be the worst." Mr. Hayes had been berating Adam for the past five minutes straight. We were back in his office, sitting in those same chairs. For a second I could almost believe it was still yesterday, if it weren't for the pain in my jaw. "Coach Miller is going to have my head for this, but unless you can think of a *very* good reason for me not to, I'm going to have to suspend you."

"It wasn't his fault." I immediately regretted saying it. Talking hurt a *lot* right then.

"What?" Mr. Hayes and Adam said in unison. Their disbelief sounded so identical I almost laughed. Almost.

"I moved forward at the last minute. I wasn't supposed to. We'd practiced this for weeks, but I got a little carried away and stepped forward. And BAM, right in the jaw. Stupid mistake, really. That's what I get for being a little *too* into character, you know? Didn't hit my mark, though Adam hit his perfectly. All my fault." I realized I was babbling, so I snapped my jaw shut, getting another wave of pain for my effort.

"What are you saying, Mr. O'Connor?"

"It was a fake punch. Or it was supposed to be. Thought it'd be hilarious. We had this whole routine worked out. I was even gonna break a chair over Adam's back, just like in pro wrestling." I could feel Adam staring at me, but I kept my eyes fixed on Mr. Hayes. "No one knew, not even Kai. It was going to be the best practical joke ever. No one was supposed to realize it was fake until the chair bit. We'd have been the coolest kids in school."

Mr. Hayes passed his hands in front of his eyes and sighed. "Fighting is no laughing matter, Mr. O'Connor."

"Oh, I get that now, sir. Hindsight is twenty-twenty, right? It was just a stupid drama-club bet, see who could do the most convincing scene in public. Thought for sure I'd win; no one would suspect I'd team up with Adam. Heck, maybe I'll still win. Do you think a real punch disqualifies me?"

Mr. Hayes studied me intensely. I think he was waiting for me to break, start laughing—something that would give away that I was lying. I kept my face serious.

Finally he relented. "Alright, Mr. Anderson. Looks like you're off the hook. Next time, though, you might want to use a little bit more common sense when it comes to what's appropriate for the lunchroom."

"Thank you, Mr. Hayes. I will." He left.

"I don't know what you're playing at, Dylan—"

"I don't know what you mean, sir."

"—and I don't want to know. I said I'd give you detention if you got into any more shenanigans with Adam, and I meant it." I winced. This was exactly what I needed today. To my surprise, however, Mr. Hayes smiled. "But it looks like you've gotten enough punishment for your foolishness already."

"Oh, I have. Honest." I said with a laugh, which only hurt a little. I'd figured out the trick of talking without moving my jaw very much. I probably sounded more than a little mumbly. I stood up to leave, but Mr. Hayes stopped me at the door.

"Oh, Dylan," he said, "next time I see you across my desk, consequences will be dire."

Outside the principal's office, I found Adam waiting for me. He didn't say anything, though, just fell into step beside me as I made my way to my locker. He kept glancing around the halls as though expecting someone to jump out and catch him at something—hanging out with me, I guess—but class had already started, and the halls were empty.

Finally, he opened his mouth to speak, stopped himself, looked back at Mr. Hayes's door, saw it was closed, and said, "Why did you do that for me?"

I was surprised to realize that I didn't even need to think about the answer. I had acted on instinct back there, without really knowing why. But something about the way Adam asked—I'd never heard him speak so softly before, so completely without scorn—made me realize in an instant.

"We've known each other since kindergarten, Adam. In all that time, you've called me names, fired spitballs at me, shoved my head in a toilet once, and you gave me wedgies for a week until I convinced everyone you were secretly gay and just wanted your hand down my pants. You've tripped me. You've pinched me. You've dumped things in my locker. But you have never, ever hurt me." I stopped walking, turned to Adam. He refused to meet my eye. "See, I think I did something wrong. Crossed some unwritten line of our little back-and-forth. I have no idea what that line was—

the whole lunch seems like a blur to me right now—but I think I must have crossed it."

Adam met my gaze for a second and looked away. He nodded. "It's not entirely your fault. I haven't been myself lately."

Wow. Was that magnanimity, from *Adam*? "Listen, if you ever need someone to talk to…." What was I even saying?

Adam laughed bitterly. "Yeah, like I could trust you. Anything I told you, you'd just throw back in my face, probably in front of everyone."

I bristled at the accusation. Sure, I liked poking fun at Adam—who wouldn't?—but I'm not cruel. "Last December, you were a superdouche." Adam gave me an annoyed look and started to interrupt. "Let me finish. I saw you go into the bathroom down by the band room, so I followed you in to, I dunno, tell you that you had a stupid face or something. It was probably really clever. But when I opened the door, I heard something I never expected. I heard crying." Adam was staring at me. It seemed he remembered the day. "There was no one else in the bathroom, I'm sure of it. I shut the door as quietly as possible, so you wouldn't know you'd been heard, and I left. I have never, until right this second, told anyone about that. And I certainly haven't thrown it in your face to score cheap points. I'm not that guy. I *am* a good listener, however. Besides—" I smiled. "I already hate you, so you don't have to worry about what I think, unlike with your friends."

Adam was giving me an inscrutable look. "Why do you care all of a sudden?"

I shrugged. "I've always cared—hated, yes, but that's still caring. Hating you has been one of the most constant things in my life. I'd be lying if I said I didn't look forward to our verbal sparring every day. Over the summer, I write insults on note cards to prepare for the school year. I guess I just—" I hesitated. "—don't want to lose that, okay?"

For the barest fraction of a second, it looked like Adam was going to open up to me. But then the bell rang, the halls flooded with students, and the spell was broken. His face hardened, and he practically ran in his haste to get away from me.

"Weird," I said aloud, to no one in particular. Were Adam and I almost becoming friends? I laughed at the thought. Of course not. This was *Adam* we were talking about here. At best we were negotiating a truce.

CHAPTER THREE

AFTER SCHOOL there was a drama club meeting. Nothing important was discussed; it was mostly a chance for us all to hang out, sometimes play some improv games. For probably the first time, I found I didn't really want to be there. Not only did my jaw hurt, but I was too distracted; I couldn't seem to focus on anything. Eventually I just sat in the back of the auditorium and waited. Kai was my ride home, so I couldn't leave. Whenever anyone would ask why I wasn't participating—I'm usually the life of the party—I'd point to my jaw and wince dramatically for effect.

Finally four thirty rolled around, and even the most die-hard drama kids were ready to go home. We all sat outside in the grass surrounding the auditorium as, one by one, parents came to pick up their kids. Soon it was just me, Mel, and Kai, waiting for Mel's parents to show up. They had this bad habit of not showing up until well after five, but also forbade Mel from riding in any other kid's car. They didn't even trust Kai. Or, perhaps, *especially* didn't trust Kai. Even my two best friends seemed to believe that my silence stemmed from my jaw pain, so they let me sit in solitude.

"Tom was saying we're going to be doing another musical," Mel said.

"Oh God, that means we'll all have to deal with Bitch Kathy acting like a diva again," Kai complained, lying on his back in the grass. Mel punched him. "I mean, if you don't get the lead, of course. Who knows? They could choose *Screeching Harpy, the Musical.*" She punched him again, laughing despite herself.

I watched a car start driving over from the direction of the football field. When he heard it approach, Kai sat up, probably thinking it was Mel's parents. It was obviously not their car. The window rolled down. It was Adam.

"Get in," he said, looking right at me.

Kai scoffed. "Yeah right. Like that's going to happen."

"Come to think of it," Mel said, her voice dripping in sarcasm, "Dylan could use a matching bruise on the other side of his jaw."

Adam gave no sign that he heard them. He just kept looking at me, waiting. So I stood up and walked over.

"Dude, you can't seriously be thinking about going with him." Kai jumped up and grabbed my arm. "He's probably going to murder you and use your skull as a football helmet."

Normally Kai's attempts at humor would at least make me smile, but right then it just annoyed me. "Well, when they find my body, you'll know who did it. Case closed." I got in the car and slammed the door. Through the window, I said, "I'll call you tonight." Kai was staring at me like I'd sprouted wings and started breathing fire. Mel was giving me that narrow-eyed look she got when she thought she'd figured something out. I rolled up the window, and Adam drove off.

He didn't say anything. I didn't either. What could I say? Clearly he'd chosen to take me up on my offer. Well, if he wanted someone to listen, then I'd listen. But as the silence stretched on and on, I began to get a little uncomfortable. He didn't even have the radio going to relieve the monotony. There were only the sounds of the car and the wind rushing by. I looked over at Adam, but he kept his eyes firmly on the road ahead of him, his jaw clenched so tight I could see his cheek muscles popping. Out my window I noticed we were getting to the edge of town.

Okay, so maybe I hadn't quite thought this through. Where were we even going? To Adam's house? It dawned on me I had no idea where exactly that was. We weren't headed toward a coffee shop or anything; the only buildings we were passing were houses, and those were becoming fewer and farther between. I thought about asking Adam where we were, but I stopped myself. He seemed to be working something out in his head, arguing with himself. So I decided to wait.

I didn't need to wait much longer. We had entered a small wooded area, the road becoming all long and winding. Eventually the woods cleared a bit, leaving an open area maybe twenty yards across overlooking a small lake. There were no houses on the lake. This spot seemed to be totally secluded. *A perfect spot for a murder*, Kai's voice whispered in the back of my head. I ignored it. Adam pulled off the road—there was a patch of gravel, looked like it was meant for a few cars to park on. Without even bothering to turn off the car, Adam threw open his door, forcefully enough to make me jump slightly, got out, and immediately started pacing in front of the car.

I sat there, not quite knowing what to do. Left and right he went. Back and forth. I watched him through the windshield. He stepped quickly, almost violently, hands shoved in his pockets. Even from where I sat, I could see he was breathing heavily. He didn't look like he was going to slow down any time soon, or get back into the car. Maybe this was his secret place where he went to be alone for a while, do his thinking.

That was an odd thought: an introspective Adam. But it made a weird sort of sense. And where better to go when you needed to talk to someone, especially when you didn't want anyone to know that you were even with that person?

So I got out of the car, walked around to the front, leaned against the hood, and waited. Adam kept pacing furiously, but occasionally glanced my way. Abruptly, he stopped and turned to me, looking like he didn't know how to begin. Finally, instead of speaking, he pulled off his shirt.

I think I gasped then. His ribs were covered in fading bruises. "Ima go out on a limb and say those aren't from football practice, are they?" I asked quietly.

"I need you to know he's a good dad," Adam replied through clenched teeth. He opened his mouth like he was about to say more, but instead spun around, walked off to the center of the clearing, and stood, staring out at the lake. A second later I followed, stood next to him. For a minute we were both silent, watching the gentle waves.

"He left, Sunday night. After…." Adam trailed off, gesturing vaguely at his ribs. I suddenly remembered how he'd sat in Mr. Hayes office with his arms crossed. At the time I thought he looked sullen; looking back it seemed like he was protecting himself, cradling his bruised ribs.

"He's not usually like this," Adam continued. "It's been really hard on him, Mom being in the hospital again. He's just so angry." He quivered with nervous energy. Unshed tears stood in his eyes. He started pacing again. "I don't know what to do now. It's just me and my brother. Pete dropped out of school, said he'll figure everything out, but I just don't know. I don't know how we're supposed to pay the bills. *I don't know what I'm supposed to do.*"

I stopped Adam with a hand on his arm and drew him into a hug. I didn't think about it—he just seemed in so much pain. He tensed up at first. For a second I thought he'd push me away, start yelling at me. But instead he relaxed and sank to his knees. I sat next to him and held him while he cried, clinging to me like I was the only thing keeping him from drowning.

Maybe I was.

"YOU'RE GOING to need to turn right up here," I said, breaking the silence of the drive back into Oak Lake. We hadn't spoken since Adam had pulled away, wiping his eyes and clearing his throat. Together we had sat and watched the sun set past the trees.

"I remember," he said, taking the turn.

"You remember? When have you ever been to my house?"

"Seventh grade, for your birthday party."

"Oh right," I laughed, remembering. "I invited you so I could dare you to spend the night in that old house everyone thought was haunted."

"And I double dared you to come with me. Then Tony dared Derek, Derek dared Malachi…."

"And suddenly everyone was going. Yeah, how did I not see that coming?"

He chuckled. "'Cause you're an idiot."

"In my defense, I was convinced you'd be too scared to follow through."

"Me? Scared? You were the one with the girly screams every time the floor creaked, pussy boy."

"And you, big, strong jock that you are, pissed yourself 'cause you were having so much fun?" Adam began grumbling excuses under his breath: someone spilled water on him, it was just a shadow, there wasn't a working bathroom in the house anyway. They were all the same ones he'd given that night. "I planned that whole thing just to humiliate you in front of everyone," I continued, "but everyone was having too much fun to notice. See, this is what I was saying before: our hatred has only ever led to good things."

"Except this." Adam reached across the car and, gently, with the tips of his fingers, touched my jaw where he had punched me. "I never actually said sorry for that."

Well, this had gotten awkward really quickly. Was I getting my cheek caressed? Was this seriously a thing that was happening? "Uhhhhh, yeah. Don't worry about it… I guess." Adam suddenly seemed to realize what he was doing and snatched his hand away. We returned to silence, only this time, instead of being oddly comfortable, it had gained the level of awkward I had been expecting this whole trip to have. Like it had taken that weird, almost intimate, gesture to suddenly remind us both who we were, and just how weird what we were doing really was. I think we had forgotten for a moment.

Luckily, we were saved from any further awkwardness. After maybe two minutes, Adam pulled into my driveway, and I was quick to hop out of the car.

"Hey, Dylan?" Adam said.

I stopped, half in and half out of the car. "Yeah?"

"You're not gonna…. I mean, what just happened…." He licked his lips nervously. "You're not gonna… tell anyone that I—"

"That you have a stupid face, and I hate it? Sure, I'll keep mum, but I think they already know."

He smiled at me then, one of those rare, pure smiles. I'd never actually seen him smile at *me* that way before. It made his face seem warm, which was weird, 'cause it was Adam, and made a weird ache appear in my chest, which was gross, *'cause it was Adam.*

"Thanks," he said, sounding really sincere. Which sucked, 'cause that meant I'd be a superdouche if I made some sarcastic comment to hide this weird feeling I was suddenly having. So instead I shrugged and shut the door.

Worst of all, he kept smiling.

I found twenty-two texts from Kai on my phone, demanding to know if I was dead. I decided to ignore them and let him stew a bit. I texted Mel, though. She was less funny when she worried. Like, "they'd find Adam's body in the morning" less funny.

I'm home. Not dead.

She responded almost immediately. *You okay?*

Yeah. Weird night.

I'll bet.

CHAPTER FOUR

KAI'S ROOM was filled with the sound of gunshots. His mom wasn't home, so we were there alone and felt no need to turn the volume down. We lay side by side on his bed, PlayStation controllers in hand, doing our very best to murder each other with a wide array of virtual guns and explosives. You know, best friend stuff.

"When's Mel getting here?" I asked, raising my voice over the screams of the dying.

"Oh, she's not coming. I figured it's been so long since we've hung out, just the two of us, so I didn't invite her."

It had been too long since Kai and I had spent much time together without Mel. Months, in fact. Every time Kai and I made plans over the summer—even when I dropped some not-so-subtle hints we should have a bros' night in—Mel always ended up being invited, and Kai would shoot me those "I'm innocent, don't hate me" eyes. I guess you can't compete with a girl, you know? Sometimes I wished it weren't Mel, so I could hate her for being that bitch who keeps getting between us. But she's my best friend too, so I can't. Ironically, Mel and I have found plenty of time to hang out without Kai, but then she's not the one with the massive crush. So I had a feeling I knew what this sudden desire for a Saturday alone was all about.

"Sooooo," Kai said after a moment. "What have you and Adam been spending all that time talking about?"

I knew it. It had been a week and a half since Adam picked me up after school that Wednesday, and since then we'd hung out four more times. Mel and Kai wanted to know what was going on, of course, and I told them that Adam just needed to talk about some stuff, and they couldn't tell anyone even that much. Which was the truth. Adam had a *lot* he'd needed to talk about. At his clearing overlooking the lake, Adam started spilling his heart to me, in little fits and starts at first, but it had gotten to the point where we'd have long conversations about family, school, life in general. His mom had been diagnosed with breast cancer the year before—that's what I'd caught him crying about in the bathroom—and they thought she'd beaten it. But over the summer, they discovered it had migrated to other parts of her body, which made it a lot harder to treat. Right before school started, she had been admitted to the hospital, where she'd been for almost a month now. That was also when his dad had started drinking and getting really angry. But he'd never hit Adam, not until that Sunday, when he beat his son and left.

It was a crazy experience, seeing a softer side of Adam. He talked about wanting to go to college, which I had no idea he was even thinking about. I guess I always assumed he was just some dumb jock and didn't care about education. Only he didn't know if he'd be able to now. His older brother Pete was basically supporting them both, though they had gotten a check in the mail from their dad. But Adam was worried that those would stop soon. And I knew he'd do whatever it took to make sure his mom's hospital bills got paid. He talked about football too, how he didn't want the team to think he was weak. How the coach expected so much of him, but he was afraid he wasn't gonna be able to deliver now. He talked about feeling alone, having no one to talk to. At least before I came along.

Basically a bunch of really personal stuff. "I can't really tell you." I could *feel* the sulk vibrating off him. "Unless you want to invoke Best Friend Privilege and force me to break my bond of trust."

"No," Kai grumbled, "you can have your stupid secrets." He sighed, dropped his controller and stood up. "Let's go swimming," he said as he pulled off his shirt and crossed to the other side of the room to his closet.

"Now? It's kinda cold out."

"Fine. We can go in the hot tub. Wuss." He threw his pants at me, hitting me in the back of the head.

I kept my eyes focused diligently on the TV screen. The last thing I needed in life was to accidentally fall in lust with my best friend. We already cared for each other more than a little bit. Kai had never been sparing with his affection, and he'd been telling me he loved me since middle school, but he was still straight, so it was important my feelings didn't stray too far from the platonic. And once you'd seen someone's dick, you could never quite look at them the same way. I learned that the hard way—*Oh, James P. Hogan, the way that soapy water cascaded down your every divine contour in that locker room of destiny. I know you caught me staring, but you only smiled that perfect smile and....* Dammit, see what I mean? Unfortunately, Kai had always been really comfortable around me, so I'd always had plenty of temptation. When I came out to him, I had hoped that might curb his enthusiasm a bit. And it had. For about a week. Then it was back to showering with the door open and shedding clothes without a care in the world.

Or pausing to admire himself in the mirror, which I was pretty certain he was doing now, if the occasional reflection in the TV was anything to go by.

"Hey, Dylan, I need your opinion on something."

"What's that?" I swear to God, if he expects me to help him pick out the right swimsuit, like our friendship were some episode of *Queer Eye for the Straight Guy*....

"Look," he said, so I turned around. Big mistake. "Do you think my dick's too small?"

Remember that hotness scale I was discussing before? Well, Kai falls in solidly at number three. He's the textbook definition of tall, dark, and handsome. And while lots of other guys rely on copious amounts of exercise to maintain their spots on the scale, Kai's abs were all genetics. And, it turns out, that wasn't the only gift his parents had given him. For the first time in our long friendship, I got a pure, unadulterated look at Kai's junk. It took a nanosecond for my eyes to hone in, and now they were trapped. I couldn't look away. His cock wasn't huge, it was probably even a little shy of average, but what it lacked in bulk it made up for in beauty. His package dangled, perfectly symmetrical, below his neatly trimmed bush. His balls hung heavily, in ideal proportion to his circumcised shaft. His dick was art—da Vinci could have used Kai to model the Vitruvian Man.

It felt like a semitruck had crashed into my gut.

"I'll take that as a no," Kai said with a decidedly wicked little laugh.

"Please put some pants on." I said. I *did not* moan.

"Is that really what you want, Dylan?" Kai shook his hips from side to side, making his cock flop about luridly. My own dick jumped, and that time I *might* have moaned. "Thought not," he said.

Slowly my brain started to catch up to what was happening. Which is to say, it started to remind me that maybe I shouldn't be staring at my best friend's junk, drooling. It also began to wonder just what exactly was going on here, and what I was supposed to do. Kai, however, seemed hell-bent on keeping me from getting my footing.

"You love me, right?"

"What?" Hard as I tried, I couldn't catch my breath enough to say that above a whisper.

"'Cause I love you," Kai continued, not seeming to hear me. "And I've been thinking… like, I'm horny all the time, and you probably are too. We're teenagers, right? I don't know about you, but I masturbate, like, whoa. And since we already love each other…. I mean, there's really only one way for us to get any closer… and how do I know I'm not gay anyway, without trying? I already like you more than anyone else."

"What are you…?" I had to stop, search for my voice, and try again. "What are you trying to say?"

He cocked his head to the side, hands on his hips. "I'm asking if you want to suck my dick, dude."

My brain finally quit trying to catch up. It threw up its little brain-hands and went into a back room somewhere to watch TV. In its defense, I don't think it was getting anywhere near enough blood right then to have even a fighting chance. I finally managed to tear my eyes away from Kai's downstairs magic, only to stare up at his face, my jaw hanging open, with a dumb look of incomprehension. Kai giggled a little at my confusion—was he nervous?—and stepped right up to the bed, until his cock was literally in my face.

Tentatively, I reached out my hand, cupped his balls and lifted ever so slightly, feeling the weight of his junk in my hands.

It was amazing.

Kai didn't slap my hand away, laughing at me for falling for some elaborate prank, which, I realized, a huge part of me had been expecting. I lifted a little higher, until his dick was a fraction of an inch from my lips. My tongue darted out and, delicately, I licked the tip. This time, it was Kai who moaned. *This is really happening*, I thought and, inhibition suddenly evaporating, I gave into years of pent-up desire and swallowed his cock.

In seconds, Kai was hard in my mouth. I massaged his balls with my hand as I worked, gaining confidence and speed. Kai's moans became louder until they drowned out the sounds of the video game, unpaused but forgotten. Suddenly, I felt his hands grab my head, fingers clutching at my hair. He shoved my head down, thrusting over and over, his cock working deeper as he fucked my face. He did it with a force and an intensity I was totally unprepared for, and I gagged.

I pulled away, and Kai laughed at me, teasing, "Come on, dude. Take it like a man."

I laughed too, and punched him softly in the stomach. Honestly, I was glad for the break, if only because it gave me the opportunity to look again at Kai's entire body. Hard, his dick had grown exponentially; it stood straight and tall, throbbing. Kai grabbed his cock and stroked it slowly, twice, along the entire length of his shaft. I growled with desire.

I leapt up and pushed Kai down onto the bed. Kneeling on the floor, I found myself in a much better position to devour his cock. His legs were spread wide to admit me, and the hand I used to massage his balls began working its way farther down. I found what I was looking for, took his cock as deeply as I could without gagging, and at the same instant thrust my middle finger into Kai's asshole.

"Dude!" Kai yelped. I could feel his whole body tense around my finger. "What the fuck are you…." but right then I found it. His prostate was a little harder for me to find than my own was, but the second I stroked it, Kai's words dissolved into shouts of pleasure. I went faster, tongue swirling the head of his cock, one hand massaging his insides, the other his balls, which had begun to draw up close to his body. His ass tightened around my finger, gripping it. His breath came in ragged, heaving gasps.

"Dylan." Kai moaned. "I'm going to...."

But I knew what was coming, and I was prepared for it. Kai's ass clenched so hard I was almost afraid it would snap my finger. He thrust up, forcing his cock deep, and with a yell, he filled my mouth with his cum, hot and salty. It hit the back of my throat, but I fought the urge to gag—I was getting pretty good at that. I swallowed every last drop, sucked him dry through spurt after spurt until finally he was empty. I licked him clean, popped my finger out of him, and flopped down beside him on the bed, listening to him catch his breath.

Suddenly I became painfully aware of my own needs. The front of my shorts were stained with precum, and I was so hard, it hurt.

Kai noticed too. "Dude, little Dylan's straining to escape his prison. Let him out, man." But when I reached down to unbutton my pants, he grabbed my arm, stopping me. "I guess there's gotta be a little quid pro quo, eh, buddy?" He slid off the bed, knelt between my legs, unbuttoned my shorts, and tugged them off. I pulled off my shirt and put my hands behind my head, propping myself up for a better view. My bush was the same dark red as my hair, and more wild than Kai's had been, and my dick was longer—though, it seemed to me, less immaculately shaped. Freed from my shorts, it flopped against my stomach with a wet smack, which made Kai giggle. Definitely nervous this time.

He grabbed my cock and slowly started jerking it. He quickly began to go faster. The sight of him there, head just beyond my cock, tongue caught between his teeth in concentration, made my heart skip a beat. *This is really happening!* I hadn't even let myself dream of this possibility, but now it was right there before me. Touching me. Kai covered his face with his other hand, as if embarrassed or unable to believe this was happening too. He looked up at me through his fingers, saw me watching him, and winked. I shuddered. Seeing the effect he had on me gave Kai confidence. He began to work my cock harder, stroking from base to tip instead of awkward, rapid jerking. He grinned at me wickedly as my moans filled the room, and laughed every time I gasped his name. With a mischievous glint in his eye, he brought his face closer to my cock, and my breath caught. His tongue darted out, and I thought I would die. He ran the tip of his tongue along the entire length of my shaft, and it was too much. I burst, hot ribbons of cum blasting onto my chest, my neck, and even beyond, spraying Kai's bed with the evidence of my pleasure. I had never cum so hard in my life.

Kai got into bed next to me, laid his head on my chest, and said, "That was actually kinda fun." In seconds he was asleep. I wasn't far behind.

I HAD the most remarkable dream. In it, Kai and I had been naked, fooling around. Then we lay enfolded in each other's arms, him holding me close as he whispered in my ear, *I love you.* I floated in that in-between of waking and sleeping, where you were still dreaming but knew it was fake and you were about to wake up. But I wanted so desperately to stay there forever, because in real life....

My eyes snapped open.

Wait, some of that had actually happened. I looked over and, sure enough, Kai was lying there naked, curled into a ball on the complete opposite side of the bed, his back to me. It wasn't the postcoital snuggle of my dreams, but we were still naked, and I was covered in dried cum. And I could remember the taste of his.

All I could think, as I watched him sleep, was the sight of him standing there, naked and erect, or holding my dick in his hand. I felt an ache, deep in my gut, to crawl across the bed and hold him close, feel his heartbeat against mine. Instead I rolled out of the bed, looking for my clothes and a way to escape before Kai woke up and everything was ruined. He might love me, but this could tip me off the edge into falling *in* love with him.

But Kai stirred before I could do more than stand up. He rolled over and smiled tiredly at me, taking in my naked body through heavy-lidded eyes. His look held no disgust or regret, or any of the things I had been fearing he'd feel if he woke up to find us naked together.

Instead he only said, "Good morning, starshine," even though the sun was clearly setting outside. He stretched, bringing his cock back into my line of sight. Once again I experienced that tunnel vision of desire, where the whole world disappeared except Kai—more specifically the bit between his legs. Kai began playing with himself, distractedly, his grin growing wider as he noted the effect he had on me.

"Dylan, dude, you're covered in dried cum. Gross. We should take a shower."

I thought for a second I was imagining things. Surely this was all a dream, right? "We?"

"Mmhmm," he said, getting out of bed. He grabbed me by the hips and steered me toward the bathroom.

Why had I wanted to leave again?

I was hard before we even got in the shower, which Kai apparently found hilarious. He draped a washcloth over my cock, laughing, making jokes about pitching tents. It started off as less a sexual shower and more a playful one, with Kai giggling throughout, spraying me with cold water, initiating more than one soap fight and staying decidedly flaccid. But I did get to rub soap onto his back, and when I let my cock brush against his ass, he giggled but didn't make me stop. Finally, I dropped all pretense, reached around and grabbed his dick, stroking it until he was hard in my hand. He leaned back against me, thrusting into my hand, each movement of his hips rubbing his ass against my cock. Soon he came, but when I had milked every last drop from him, he kept moving, caressing my dick with his ass. I had the strange feeling that shoving my finger in his ass earlier had awakened some desire in him, something I definitely wanted to explore. Holding him tight against me, I started thrusting until I came, covering his back and my abs with cum.

"Oh, dude, gross. Now you have to wash my back again." He giggled. "And this time only washing."

The shower finished pretty quickly after that. I tried to dry him off, but he kept whipping me with a towel, turning the tender moment I had imagined into more of a locker room struggle. Then we played some more video games and went to bed. I slept on the inflatable mattress Kai had under his bed. I kept hoping he'd tell me to crawl in bed with him, but he never did, and something stopped me from asking if I could. Before I could muster the courage, he was snoring. Soon I fell asleep with that weird ache in my gut.

CHAPTER FIVE

IN BIOLOGY class, Mel sat between Kai and me, eyes shifting suspiciously back and forth, first at me, then at Kai. I pretended not to notice. Mel was always unusually perceptive, and it was clear she knew something had happened. For one thing, she never sat *between* us. She had often made fun of Kai and me, saying we were attached at the hip. But, perhaps most incriminating, neither of us said anything. Our usually incessant joking banter was completely absent. Worse, this had been going on for days now: the awkward silences, keeping our distance, refusing to look at each other.

"Okay, one of you better start telling me what is going on," she said through clenched teeth.

Kai looked up from the paper he was idly doodling on. "What?"

"You know exactly what I mean. You two have barely spoken all week. Are you fighting about something? What?"

"We're not fighting, are we, Dylan?"

I looked over and, for a second, our eyes met, Kai's and mine. In that instant, a thousand images flashed through my mind: Kai naked, me blasting load after load of cum onto his chest, his hand holding my cock, his face at the moment of orgasm. We both looked away.

"Nope. Definitely not fighting." I said, feeling my face turn red.

Mel narrowed her eyes and stared hard at me, as though trying to make me break through sheer force of will. Angrily she said, "Well, whenever you two decide you want to start talking to me, let me know." She stood up, using the pretense of needing to throw something away, and sat back down at a different table.

I stole another look at Kai, but if he noticed, he didn't look up from his doodling. Even the sight of his bent neck, ignoring me, was enough to make me hard, remembering the things we'd done and imagining what else I'd like to do.

The truth was, I wanted to tell Mel what was happening. Only, I wasn't entirely sure what it was myself. Almost every night, Kai would come to my house, or I to his, the clothes would come off, and the sexual Olympics would resume. I'd given Kai more blow jobs than I could count—that's a lie: the answer was eight, and I could vividly recall each and every one—but the most Kai ever did for me was a quick hand job. Occasionally he would let me rub my dick between his ass cheeks until I came. We never kissed. Never slept together, as in actual sleep. And at school, things kept getting more and more awkward. I'd just sit there with this ache in my gut, unable to look at him without wanting to jump him right there in front of everyone—and I couldn't help but feel that Kai didn't want anyone to know, even Mel.

Maybe especially Mel.

However, all this week, in strange juxtaposition to the strain in my relationship with Kai, Adam and I were becoming almost friends. Which isn't to say we were being nice to each other, quite the opposite actually. If anything, there were even *more* insults yelled down the hall, or dramatic showdowns in the lunchroom. Only now, they had been sapped of all malice. Adam never called me a faggot anymore, though several iterations of "fairy" did make a routine appearance, there was never a threat of violence, and more often than not we walked away laughing at some clever thing the other had said. We had become almost playful.

I hadn't seen Adam outside of school this week, though. It was possible he'd shown up at the auditorium looking for me, but I hadn't ever been there to find out. Kai and I had been rushing off right after school, not even bothering to wait with Mel for her parents to pick her up.

"Kai," I whispered. He grunted acknowledgement but didn't even glance at me. "We're not fighting, are we?"

He did look up then, briefly. "No. What makes you think that?"

"Nothing, it's just…." But he was already back to his doodles.

After school, Kai seemed to be in an unusual hurry to get back to his car. I lagged behind a bit. I guess I wanted to see if Kai would stop, wait up, maybe ask me what was wrong. As the day had gone by, with Kai still distant, I had started to have a lot of misgivings about this… thing we had together. Sure, I had been gaining the Kai of my dreams, but I'd begun to worry it was at the expense of Kai-my-best-friend. And I wasn't sure I wanted that. I wasn't sure what I wanted, really.

"Yo, fairy boy." I jumped, surprised. I hadn't noticed Adam's car pull up alongside me. Adam laughed. "Are all fairies that scared of a real man?"

"I don't know. When I meet a real man, I'll let you know." I was smiling despite myself. Adam was cheering me up when Kai had got me down. Was the whole world backward?

"You free tonight?" Adam asked. "I was thinking we could…."

Kai appeared out of nowhere and slung his arm around my shoulder protectively. "He's busy. We've got plans."

Adam looked at me. His eyes were hard, almost penetrating. Before I could answer, however, Adam drove off.

"That was close," Kai said. He grabbed my hand and pulled me the last fifteen feet or so to his car. Despite everything, I found I was disappointed when he let go.

We drove in silence for a while. I wasn't certain how to articulate what I was feeling. Kai was the first to break the silence.

"I feel like I need to apologize," he said.

"Oh?"

"Mel was right. Things have been weird at school. It's just… I can't stop thinking about…."

"About what?" I asked. I mean, I knew perfectly well what he couldn't stop thinking about. I wanted to hear him say what he thought this was, between him and me.

"About this." He grabbed my hand and put it on his crotch. I could feel him, rock hard, straining against his jeans.

Okay, so it wasn't quite the heart-to-heart I had been hoping for, but I still felt better. At least now I knew his awkwardness at school wasn't some sign of a growing divide between us. I guess, just like me, he was too caught up in sexual fantasy to function quite right at school. Smiling, I unbuttoned his jeans and slipped my hand under the waistband of his boxers. Kai grabbed my leg, fingers digging into my thigh.

God, I could put up with any amount of awkwardness for this.

Unfortunately, Kai didn't live too far from school, so we didn't get a chance to get very creative. Or maybe that was a good thing. Kai was *driving*, after all. I can just imagine the look on the cop's face, unable to pull our dead bodies from the wreckage 'cause our hands were too far down each other's pants—it would make an *excellent* obituary. Kai had to shove himself back into his jeans, which proved to be a lot harder than it was to get him out. Trying to look casual as we held our backpacks in front of our crotches, we ran inside. Kai did a quick snoop around his house to make sure his mom wasn't home. He still locked the door to his bedroom however.

I was anxious to start. We usually began with me giving Kai a blow job, but Kai didn't rush to take his clothes off. Instead, he reached under his bed, and pulled out a brown paper bag. Then he tore off his clothes, threw himself on his bed, and started jacking off, watching me intently.

"Take off your clothes," he commanded. As he said it, he plunged a finger into his ass.

I ripped the seams of my shirt in my haste to get it off. Kai thrust his finger in and out. I tore off my pants, and Kai added a second finger. God, it was hot. I fell to the floor in front of him, taking his cock deep into my mouth.

"Finger me," he said. I found his prostate and stroked it with my finger. "More," he moaned, and I added another finger until he was gasping. "More," he cried, and with three fingers, I fucked his hole.

He grabbed my head, pulling me off his cock. "Open the bag," he said.

I continued to fuck him with one hand. With the other, I upended the brown paper bag, spilling its contents onto the bed. It had been filled with condoms and lube.

"I want you to fuck me."

I faltered for a second, unable to believe my ears. "Fuck me," he said again. I got to my feet, ripped open a condom and put it on.

Kai watched me, running his hands over his chest, his abs, his cock. I covered my hands in lube. I had no idea how much to use, and I didn't want to hurt Kai. I smeared lube onto his hole with one hand and my dick with the other. Satisfied we were slippery enough, I pressed the head of my cock right against Kai.

Our eyes met. We were both breathing heavily and, up till then, had been moving almost frantically. But in that moment, time seemed to slow. Kai bit his lip. He looked worried, like he didn't know if it would hurt, but in his eyes I thought I saw a need. The same need I felt.

Slowly, I pushed in. I heard Kai gasp, felt him tense around my cock, eliciting a shout of pleasure from me. He relaxed, and I slid all the way in. The feeling was intense, indescribable. Kai's face was contorted into a grimace—whether of pleasure or pain, I could not tell.

"Are you okay?" I asked him.

"Don't stop" was all he said.

I pulled out, then thrust back in. Slowly at first, but then faster and faster. I settled into a steady rhythm, hips pumping, Kai's room filling with the sounds of flesh smacking into flesh, my grunts, and Kai's shouts of pleasure. I leaned over Kai, staring deep into his eyes. I grabbed his cock, stroking in counterpoint to my thrusts. He reached up and grabbed my chest, nails digging into my pecs. With each thrust my pleasure intensified. Nothing existed except me and Kai, our bodies, together.

"Oh God!" Kai yelled and came, filling my hand and covering his chest with his cum. Suddenly the dam broke, and I was spraying my own seed deep inside him. With each wave of his orgasm, I could feel the muscles of his ass tighten around my cock, milking it dry. Finally spent, I pulled out and collapsed, exhausted, on top of Kai.

For a while I just lay there, reveling in our closeness, the feel of his entire body beneath mine. Even with everything that had been happening, I had never expected my relationship with Kai would go to this level. I gradually began to wonder what it meant.

"I never thought a straight guy would ever let someone fuck him." I said, with special emphasis on *straight guy*. I found myself hoping he would say he had realized he wasn't straight, that all he wanted was to stay this close to me forever.

Instead he said, "It's actually not that uncommon, according to the Internet. Granted, I'm pretty sure it is usually a girl with a strap-on, but I figured I should give the real thing a try, you know?"

A try? I floundered for something to say. "Why did we use a condom? I don't have anything. You can't get pregnant or whatever. Right? Ha-ha...." I was rambling, trying to cover my hurt and disappointment.

"Gross, dude. I don't want your semen in me. Good thing too, 'cause you definitely didn't pull out, which, rude, by the way." He shoved me off him and stood up. "I'm going to take a shower. I am, you know, covered." He unlocked the door and left.

After a minute, I joined him. But it was quick, almost businesslike. Kai stepped out of the shower before I had even finished soaping up. Telling me to hurry, that his mom would be home soon, he went back to his room to get dressed.

CHAPTER SIX

I STAYED home from school the next day. It was a Friday. There were no tests or anything, so it wasn't like I was missing anything. Except soul-crushing awkwardness, that is. Kai had driven me home pretty much immediately after I had gotten out of the shower. My parents could tell that something was bothering me, but they had the good sense not to pry too hard. I'd gone to my room, skipped dinner, and I'd been in there ever since. If there had ever been a day for nothing but Netflix and video games, anything to keep me from dwelling, this was definitely it.

Someone knocked on my door. "Come in," I called.

My dad poked his head in. "How are you feeling?" he asked. I shrugged. "I take it you're not going to want to come down for dinner again tonight?" I shrugged again. "I thought not. Which is why I took the liberty of bringing some up to you." He pushed open the door and came into my room carrying a tray, which he set down on the bed next to me.

The tray had a bowl of chicken noodle soup, a grilled-cheese sandwich, and a box of tissues. Dad had to know I wasn't really sick—the man was way too smart, and I hadn't even bothered to fake a cough—but it still made me feel better to get babied a little, as if I really was sick. I thanked my dad. He left, came back about an hour later for my dishes, and left again without a word.

Night fell, and I had just turned off the TV and was about to go to bed when I heard another knock. Only this time it came from the window. My bedroom was on the first floor, so it wasn't like it was impossible, but I was still surprised. I slipped out of bed, crossed to the window, and opened it.

"Adam? What are you doing here?" I shivered at the blast of cold air. I *was* only wearing my pajama pants, after all.

"You weren't at school" was his reply. He fidgeted, hands in his pockets.

"I was sick."

"Oh." More fidgeting. "Can I come in?"

"Oh yeah, sure. Why not? Why don't I let you in the front door, and we can explain to my parents together what some strange guy is doing showing up to their gay son's bedroom in the middle of the night. What *are* you doing here?"

"I kind of meant through the window."

"There's a screen. You can't just…." But Adam reached up and effortlessly popped the screen off the window.

"They're designed to come off. You know, in case of a fire," he explained. "Can I come in?"

"Yeah, I guess." Adam climbed through the window. "But you better—" Adam popped the screen expertly back in. "—do that. Huh. I should really learn how that works." Adam leaned back against the wall, arms folded, looking around my room. It wasn't much—a TV on the dresser, a few framed pictures of me and Mel and Kai hanging on the wall, a desk covered in books. I wondered how Adam had known which window was for my room. Could he possibly remember that from my birthday party all those years ago?

"So, what's up?" I asked. Adam looked at me for a second, then looked away. Come to think of it, he had been avoiding looking at me from the minute I opened the window, looking every which way except right at me. What was going on?

Instead of answering, though, Adam pulled off his shirt. Once again, he was covered with bruises. Only this time they looked fresh.

"…Oh." I racked my brain for something better to say but came up blank. So I opened my dresser, pulled out my extra pair of pajama pants, and handed them to Adam.

"What are these for?" He stared at them dumbly.

"I'm assuming you probably don't want to go home right now. So you will stay here."

He raised his eyes to meet my gaze. He swallowed. "Thanks," he said weakly.

"Don't mention it." I turned my back deliberately so he could change. I figured he'd appreciate a little privacy. After a second, I heard the clothes-rustle sound of him changing. "You can take the bed. I'll sleep on the floor."

"No. I can't kick you out of your own bed."

"Well, I'm not going to let *you* sleep on the floor, not all bruised like that. Would you rather we share the bed?"

"I don't mind."

I turned around to give Adam the benefit of my incredulous stare, but he was back to not looking at me. He seemed very vulnerable, standing there in my red flannel pajama pants, staring listlessly at the floor. And vulnerable was a word I *never* thought I'd be using in conjunction with Adam. He clearly needed a hug, but we were shirtless, and he still called me "fairy boy." I wasn't going to push my luck.

My bed wasn't nearly as big as Kai's, and I only had the one blanket, so Adam and I were nestled in pretty close. Our arms were touching, and I realized I was tensing, waiting for some reaction. Adam didn't comment on it, though, which surprised me. I couldn't help but think of Kai who, even with all we'd done together lately, would probably have taken me up on my offer to have the bed to himself. Carefully, I relaxed, letting more of our bodies—a hip, a leg—come into contact.

"Dylan?"

"What's up?"

"I—" His voice cracked, and I realized he was holding back tears. He cleared his throat. "Nothing. It's nothing. Never mind."

I waited a bit to see if he would continue. "It's okay to cry," I said when he didn't.

"That's not what my dad would say," he muttered. "Tears are for queers." He sounded bitter.

I fought back the urge to argue, remembering the intensity in Adam's voice that first night we had hung out. *I need you to know he's a good dad.* Instead, I reached under the blanket, found Adam's hand, and gave it a squeeze. I meant it to be quick, comforting. But to my surprise, Adam clung on tightly and didn't let go. Eventually I fell asleep, our fingers still intertwined.

THIS WAS becoming a habit of mine, needing a minute after waking up to figure out what was going on. I had been dreaming I was a giant teddy bear, and now that I was awake, I couldn't shake the feeling I still was. For starters, I was really very cozy, which I had always imagined was a near-constant state for teddy bears. Then there was, of course, the arms that enfolded me, holding me against a broad, muscular chest, and the face I could feel almost nuzzled in my hair. I felt squeezed, snuggled. Exactly like a giant teddy bear.

That's Adam, I realized. Last night came back to me in a flash. *Poor guy. He did just need a hug.* I really had to pee, but I didn't want to move. For one thing, I was comfortable—it felt nice to be held. For another, I didn't want to wake Adam. For a number of reasons. He'd obviously had a rough night and could use a good night's sleep. But perhaps more pressing, I was a little worried about what would happen if he woke up and realized what position we were in. By morning he could let me go and wake up without feeling like his masculinity, or whatever, had been compromised. At the very least, I could let him think he woke up first, that I never noticed, and he could save face that way.

I checked the clock on my bedside table: 2:00 a.m. There was no way my bladder was going to be denied that long. Slowly, gently, I started to lift myself out of bed.

Immediately, Adam's arms tightened, pulling me back to him.

"Adam," I whispered, patting his arm lightly. "I have to get up." He only tightened his grip in response. I could tell by his breathing he was definitely awake. His slow, steady breaths had turned rapid, even worried. Like he'd woken from one nightmare into another. What was he afraid of? That I would leave maybe? I mean, it made some sense: his dad had left for weeks, apparently had come back just to beat him again; his mom was in the hospital, and he was probably afraid she'd soon be gone for good. It seemed a little silly—this was my room, after all; where, exactly, would I go?—but I had woken from bad dreams unable to shake them too many times myself. I knew how irrational one could be in that situation.

"I'm just heading to the bathroom."

Still no response.

I sighed, annoyed. "Would you feel better if you came with?" I felt him nod after only a brief hesitation, and he released me. I took him by the hand and led him down the darkened hall to the bathroom, careful not to make too much noise. My parents' room was upstairs, so there wasn't much of a chance of waking them, but there was always the possibility one of them had gone to the kitchen for a drink of water, or escaped to the couch to avoid the other's snores. I closed the bathroom door silently behind us before turning on the light.

Adam leaned against the sink while I used the toilet. His arms were wrapped around his chest, probably self-conscious of the bruises now that the lights were on. He kept his eyes fixed firmly on the floor. He looked sheepish standing there, and I almost laughed. It was like he had finally woken up enough to feel embarrassed about not letting me out of his sight. He peeked at me from the corner of his eye, saw me looking, and immediately averted his eyes. When I went to wash my hands, I caught him staring at me in the mirror, but if he noticed, he didn't give any sign.

I led him back to my room. This time he took my hand, which I thought was a little odd; he should already know the way back to my room, even in the dark, and by now he had to be fully awake. But I didn't say anything. We crawled back into bed. I rolled over onto my side, turning my back to him, expecting him to do the same. After all, he had to feel a little awkward about all this, right? I certainly did. But he didn't. Instead, he wrapped his arms back around me, once again holding me to him.

Okay, now I started to feel a little bit weird about this whole thing. For the first time, I thought that maybe this *hadn't* been some middream teddy-bear grab. Maybe it had been deliberate, even the first time. But why? Was he in that much need of comfort? And if so, should I be doing something? I had no idea. What—hold him?

Have him talk about his feelings? Was there something he wanted from me?

A sinking feeling suddenly landed in my gut. What if this was all some elaborate prank? It hardly seemed possible after all Adam and I had gone through, the hours spent together, opening up. But then, I'd gone through some pretty elaborate routines myself to make him look a fool. What if he was doing the same to me? But if so, what was his endgame? How was this supposed to play out? What was pretending to bare his soul to me and holding me close at night supposed to accomplish? Unless….

Right then, Adam's hand moved slightly across my chest. He brushed my nipple lightly with his thumb. A jolt of electricity shot through my spine at the contact. At first I was too stunned to think. Maybe it had been accidental? But then, a moment later, he did it again. This time he took a little more time, ran his thumb around my nipple, feeling it harden. For a second I felt the tingling feeling of arousal.

But then I got mad. I was suddenly certain all of this was a trick, some fucked-up, elaborate gaybaiting that would probably lead to him humiliating me in front of the entire school. I spun around in the bed to face him, to tell him off and stop this fiasco. A thousand and one mean things to say rose within me, but all of them died on my tongue when I saw his face.

The ambient glow of the electronics in my room glinted off his tearstained cheeks. I had no idea how long he had been crying silently, but his entire face was moist. The hand I had raised to push him away from me instead found its way to his cheek. I brushed away tears with my thumb. In his eyes I saw a confused tangle of emotions, each one seeming to struggle for dominance.

"He said it was my fault Dad left. Said if I wasn't the way I was, Dad would still be there. Then he punched me, over and over." Adam started to sob, his words broken up by gasping breaths. "But doesn't he know how hard I've tried…? My whole life I've tried…. I've never done… anything… but I've always wanted… to…." With visible effort, Adam pulled himself together, brought his breathing under control. "But it hasn't done any good. Nothing has changed. And I'm so tired of never having what I want, of living every day in pain when nothing even comes of it. I'm done pretending I don't want it. I can't. I want… I want…."

"What, Adam? What do you want?"

I felt Adam's arms tighten around me, pulling me closer until our whole bodies were touching, his face only a fraction of an inch from me. "You," he whispered. And then he was kissing me.

An instant of surprise, but then my body took over. My mouth opened, and his tongue darted in. The kiss continued, deepening, becoming more and more passionate. In seconds he was on top of me, his weight pushing me deep into the bed, his cock rubbing against mine through the fabric of our pajama pants. I wrapped my arms around him, feeling the strong muscles of his shoulders ripple as he moved. I traced the muscles down his back until I found the elastic waistband of his pants and slipped my hands inside, grabbing the firmness of his ass and squeezing. He moaned into my mouth. Longing to feel more of his body against mine, I pulled his pants down below his ass.

Suddenly there was one less layer of fabric between us. Freed from the confines of his underwear, I could feel the heavy weight of his balls on my leg, the warmth of the head of his cock as it pushed past my pajama pants and onto my abs. He broke away from the kiss, sitting up on his knees long enough to tug off my own pants and boxers with such intensity I could hear them rip. Then he was back on top of me, kissing me with renewed energy and thrusting his hips against mine.

This was different from anything that had happened with Kai. It was slower, more passionate. As our bodies rubbed against each other, our hands explored every inch. This wasn't about pleasure, though there was plenty of that—it was about a need I could tell we both felt, a need to press ourselves together so tightly we might just become one.

I have no idea how long this lasted. It could have been hours. Time had lost all meaning; everything faded into the taste of Adam's mouth and the feel of his body. But eventually things started going faster, becoming more frenzied. Our breath came in sharper, more ragged gasps between kisses as we both climbed together toward climax. And when it happened and our cum mingled together with the sweat on our pressed-together bodies, he didn't stop kissing me. The kisses became softer, more tender. The need had passed, but the desire remained. And when even that was done, we lay side by side, legs entwined and foreheads pressed together. He stared deep into my eyes, playing idly with my hair, and I traced designs on his bicep.

"You know," Adam said, "I think this would be the perfect moment… if it weren't for the feeling of cum slowly drying on my stomach."

I laughed. Without breaking out of Adam's grip, I kicked my pants off my ankles, where they had been bunched since Adam had pulled them down. I grabbed them and used them to wipe myself clean. Then I started on Adam, beginning at his chest and working my way slowly down until finally I got to his cock. I abandoned my makeshift towel. I wanted to hold Adam in my hand.

Even flaccid, his dick was huge, long and fat. Wrapping my fingers around his shaft, I felt it jump a little in response, which made me smile. Adam's eyes continued to bore into mine. His breath began to grow thick and heavy. I started to stroke, slowly, delighting in the sensation of his soft cock in my hand, feeling it begin to grow hard again. I reached my other hand down to cup his balls, which hung low, draped over his thigh. I felt his hand move down my side to my hip, but there it hesitated. I grabbed his wrist and brought it farther, until it rested on my cock. As if emboldened by my permission, his hand began to explore my junk, massaging my balls, pulling on my hardening shaft, swirling the precum around the head of my cock with his thumb. Throughout it all, we never broke eye contact.

This time I used Adam's pajama pants to clean us off before casting those too on the floor.

By then, I was exhausted. I felt Adam lightly kiss my eyelids. I hadn't realized my eyes had closed. I snuggled in closer to his chest, breathing the mingled smell of sweat, cum, and pure Adam. I realized I had this feeling, deep in my gut. But unlike the ache I had felt with Kai, this was different. It was warm.

I fell asleep with a smile on my lips, cradled in Adam's arms.

CHAPTER SEVEN

I AWOKE to the sensation of soft kisses on my collarbone.

"Good morning," Adam whispered in my ear. I could feel his morning wood pressed against my back.

"We're spooning!"

"Uh, yeah." Adam chuckled. "Obviously."

"No," I said, "I mean I just realized. Last night when I woke up, I thought... I don't know, really. That you had accidentally grabbed me in your sleep, or something, for some strange reason. But it was intentional. You were *spooning* me." I smacked my forehead. "Oh man, and the whole 'we can share the bed' bit! How did I not see through that? Last night is starting to make a *lot* more sense."

"You really didn't know? I thought you were teasing me."

I laughed. "No idea."

"I thought you knew. I'm always afraid everyone knows. That they can tell I'm...." He trailed off.

I turned so I could look at him. "It's okay," I said. "You can say it."

Knock knock knock. My room rang with the sound. Someone was at the door.

Adam's eyes grew wide, his mouth agape. "What?" I called, doing my best to make my voice sound like I had been woken up.

"Wakey wakey," my dad's voice came through the door. "Can I come in?"

I groaned loudly, a superb impersonation of it's-Saturday-let-me-sleep-in, if I do say so myself. "Let me put on pants." I said, crawling out of bed and searching around for something to throw on. Adam clutched the blankets to him and slid off the bed, falling to the floor with barely a thump. He rolled under the bed.

I found a pair of sweatpants, plastered a sleep-befuddled expression on my face, and pulled my door open.

Dad stood there, arms crossed, amused expression on his face. "Since when do you lock your door?" he asked.

"Since I started sleeping naked."

"Since when do you sleep naked?"

"Since you started turning the thermostat up to, like, ninety." Even I was a little impressed with my nonchalance, the ease of my answers.

"Uh-huh. I see." Was that a smirk on my dad's face? What did he find so funny? "Well, Mom's making waffles. Would you like any?"

"No, thanks. I think I'm going back to sleep."

"How about your friend? Would he care for any waffles?"

For a second, I thought my eyes were going to pop out of my face. At the very least my jaw was bound to fall out of its socket and hit the floor any minute now.

The silence stretched on until finally, in a teeny tiny voice, Adam said, "No, thanks, Mr. O'Connor."

The breath I didn't realize I had been holding burst out of me in a rush. "How did you know?" I asked my dad.

"I can see him under the bed. You kids should really learn how perspective works. Line of sight and whatnot. Besides, he parked his car in the driveway. Not the masters of stealth, you guys."

I heard my mother's voice drifting down the hall from the kitchen. "Ask him who it is!"

"Your mother wants to know who it is. She thinks it's that boy you played soccer with back in the sixth grade. What was his name?"

"It's not Tommy. She thinks—" I raised my voice, yelling down the hall, "You thought Tommy was gay?"

"That boy was *way* too pretty to be straight," she called back.

"For the record," my dad interjected dryly, "I don't believe that's how it works."

"I—wait. You're not mad?"

"You know, I've put a lot of thought into this over the years," Dad said.

"Wut?"

"The big reason," Dad continued, "why I'm supposed to be mad here is 'cause if you got some girl pregnant this young, you're almost guaranteed to ruin at least one life. But the whole gay thing kind of upended that logic. So really, the only real reason I can come up with to be upset here—and trust me, I have tried—is that, honestly, all this makes me feel old. Like really, *really* old. And that's not much of a reason, it seems to me. Besides, there's only so much parental hypocrisy I can handle. The veggies were one thing; this is an entirely different story."

Mom appeared at the end of the hall, stirring a bowl of waffle batter. "Yeah, your father was a real slut in high school. Like you would not believe."

Dad's grin turned wicked. "Your mother, on the other hand, didn't become a slut until college. It's amazing how many dicks I had to pull out of her before I could convince her to go out with me. At one point she was even knee-deep in pussy." Mom threw the whisk at him, which only made him laugh. They began arguing—loudly, I might add—about whose sexual adventures had been the most embarrassing.

"Gross." I closed the door to my room, shutting them out.

This was, for better or for worse, the parents I was stuck with. The two things they seemed to like best in this world were trying to one-up each other and laughing at my discomfort. Put those things together and, viola, you have one of their patented TMI fests. I actually still wonder sometimes how much of what they told me was even true, and how much was just extravagant lies for their own amusement. God knows half of what I say falls into the latter category.

Dad called through the door. "Let us know when your mystery man is ready to leave. We can all look the other way while he pretends to sneak out through the window." Mom laughed. "I could even burst in with a shotgun, shouting about despoiling my little girl." Mom was no longer laughing. No, by then it was definitely a cackle.

"Oh man," I said, turning back toward my bed. "I can't believe that just happened." Adam didn't respond. In fact, I couldn't even see Adam. He hadn't gotten up off the floor. I walked around to the other side of my bed and found him, lying still half under the bed with a look of sheer panic on his face.

Oh fuck, I thought. And he had just been telling me how scared he was of being found out. My parents: perfect timing as usual.

I fell to the floor and cradled Adam's head in my lap. "It's okay," I said. "They don't know it was you. No one will find out. I promise. You don't have to be afraid."

He smiled weakly. "I know. That was just… a little too sudden. I'm all right. Really."

He pulled himself the rest of the way out from under the bed and stood up. When he got to his feet, the blanket, which had been loosely wrapped around his body, fell to the floor. For the first time, I got to behold Adam, by the full light of day, in all his naked glory.

He stretched, at first oblivious to my wide-eyed staring. His incredibly well-defined muscles rippled under his skin. You know, I think it is entirely possible I had underestimated the worth of a well-defined musculature.

Watching the sunlight play over Adam's abs, I found myself reassessing his place in Oak Lake's hotness scale. And that wasn't even mentioning his crowning glory, the fat tool that hung between his legs under a thick, blond bush. I had noticed the night before how large it was, but I had only been going by the feel against my hip and in my hand. But looking at it now, full in the face so to speak, I was breathless. It was by far the biggest dick I had seen, outside of Internet porn videos. And his balls, refusing to be outdone, hung equally low, swaying slightly with his every movement. It was like an erotic pocket watch, swinging back and forth, hypnotizing me.

Adam finally noticed my scrutiny. For a second, he got self-conscious. His shoulders slouched slightly, and he turned away from me, growing red in the face. But this only managed to bring me the sight of even more of his body. His broad shoulders, which I had always thought made him look kind of oafish, now only furthered my arousal. But it was nothing compared to the perfection that was his ass. It was like it had been sculpted out of marble by a

Renaissance master to encapsulate the ideal behind. And through his legs I could still see his balls, dangling, enticing.

If Kai had been the Vitruvian Man, then Adam was Adonis.

He peeked over his shoulder and noticed my still rapt gaze. His blush deepened but, instead of trying to hide again, he began to flex. He started with his ass, one cheek, then the next, grinning as I gasped with desire. Then he flexed his shoulders, turning his torso to flex his arms, his pecs, even his abs, but kept his hips turned away from me, giving me only the occasional tantalizing glimpses of his cock.

Abruptly, Adam stooped and picked up the blanket, wrapping it around himself. I moaned in protest.

"This is hardly fair," he said. "After all, I still haven't had the chance to look at you." With that, he sat down at my desk, turning the chair to look at me expectantly.

Now it was my turn to be embarrassed. I mean, I didn't think I was *un*attractive or anything—quite the opposite, actually—but compared to Adam….

For one thing, everything was smaller. I was shorter, fewer muscles, smaller dick. I also lacked his healthy tan, hairless chest, and sculpted abs. Sure, I had been naked in front of Kai, but then, he had never looked at me quite like Adam was doing now. With impatience, and hunger. What if he didn't like what he saw?

Slowly, I stood up. I was still hard from Adam's show, and the front of my sweatpants bulged outward. I refused to look at Adam. Tentatively, I pulled down my pants, kicked them off, and stood there, unsure what to do. Should I do a little show like Adam had? I mean, I didn't really have many muscles worth flexing. Maybe I should, I don't know, wiggle my dick suggestively at him? Was that a thing?

I worked up the nerve to peek at Adam, to see how he was taking the sight of me by the cruel light of day. To my surprise, his eyes were wide, drinking in every inch of me.

"Wow," he said, gaze fixed firmly on my cock. He stood up, letting the blanket fall away. He too was hard, just from looking at me. I felt all self-consciousness melt away as he stepped up, grabbed me, thrust out bodies together, and began kissing me with a greater passion and intensity than ever before. I broke away and started to get down on my knees, determined to take Adam into my mouth. But he stopped me.

"Not—" He spoke, breathlessly, between kisses. "—until I—make up—for—every kiss I wanted—but was too afraid to take." I melted, just a little. Adam wrapped his hand around both our cocks, stroking them as one. I moaned. Without breaking the kiss, he grabbed me by my waist and lifted me up. I wrapped my legs around his hips, feeling his hard cock poking against my ass.

"So strong," I said, bending my head to kiss the taut muscles of his biceps. I could really get behind this whole "muscles" thing. That was becoming clearer by the second.

Adam grinned wickedly at me. He carried me across the room, dropping me onto the bed on my back. He got on top of me, arms on either side of my head holding himself above me. For a while, neither of us moved. I stared up at him, marveling at the sight of him above me, the strong muscles of his chest and arms working to hold him up, his bed-tousled hair and bright blue eyes. He stared down at me with a look I didn't understand. Almost like disbelief. I reached up to touch his cheek, feeling the hints of beard stubble.

"What is it?" I asked.

"It's strange. Seeing you like this. I've only ever looked down like this on girls…."

"Ew. Way to kill the mood there, guy."

He laughed softly. "No, I mean I usually have to imagine… a guy." He hesitated for only a fraction of a second, but I noticed it and wondered what it meant, what he had been about to say. "It's weird to actually have a guy under me."

"But good?"

He smiled so large it almost split his face in two. "Oh yeah." He dropped down onto the bed beside me, staring up at the ceiling.

The tone of the room had definitely changed. The lust and passion that had been there seconds ago seemed to have drained away, a more introspective feel replacing it. Inwardly, I raged a little, but gave no sign. Instead, I took his hand, twining our fingers together. He squeezed tightly.

"You've, uh, done this with many girls?" I asked.

"You really want to know?"

Yes. "No, I guess not."

He sighed. "I forced myself, hoping it would, I don't know, change me. I never made it this far with any girl, I couldn't make myself do it. But I had to keep up appearances."

I gave his hand a squeeze. I hooked the blanket with my foot, lifting it until I could reach it with my free hand and pull it over us. "I understand," I said, snuggling into Adam.

He snorted in disbelief. "Yeah, right."

"Um, contrary to popular belief, I did not burst out of my mother's vagina on the back of a rainbow in a cloud of glitter. I realized I was gay pretty young, but that didn't stop me from hating myself for a while. I tried to play the 'I promise I'm straight' game for almost five years. I've only been out since the eighth grade." Adam had squeezed my hand when I said I used to hate myself. It was a silent bit of protest, of reassurance. It was sweet.

"If you hated yourself for being gay, then how… I mean, why did you come out?"

"I'm not keen on dishonesty. *Especially* with myself. Plus, Kai helped me stop hating myself."

"How?"

"By telling me he cared about me. Making me realize other people cared about me. It's quite a bit more difficult to go on thinking you're worthless when people whose opinions you value keep insisting otherwise."

"Yeah. That makes sense." He sounded sad. "Malachi sounds like a good friend."

"He's the best friend."

"My friends would never have done that."

I let go of his hand to wrap my arms around him, laying my head on his chest. "I'm sorry."

He put his arm around me. "It's okay. If any of them had told me they cared about me, I probably would have punched them and called them a fag. So, I guess it's not entirely their fault." He started idly playing with my hair. "But that doesn't matter anymore. Only one more year of this and I'll be out of here. College will be a new place, with new people, I'll be able to start over."

"So you've decided you're going?" Last we'd talked about it, Adam had been torn between wanting to go and feeling like he needed to stay with his family.

"Yeah. Mom has already started picking out what schools she thinks I should go to. I'm like, Mom, I'm not going to be able to even apply until next year, but it is all she can talk about these days. It's like she thinks she won't...." He trailed off, but I knew what he had been about to say. *Like she thinks she won't be around next year.* I squeezed him a little tighter. He cleared his throat. "Anyway, the schools she's picked are way out of my league. She wants me to apply to the most prestigious universities in the country, but I'll never get in."

"Why not? Your grades are good enough."

"I guess. But I still have to take the SAT, and I'm bad at standardized tests."

It was starting to sound like Adam was making excuses, like he had already decided he was going to fail and so wasn't going to even try. There was no way I was going to let that fly.

"I'll help you."

"I don't know...."

"I'm serious. I've always been good at those. They're pretty easy once you get the knack." Adam started to say something, but I cut him off. "Listen, you can argue all you want, but I'm helping you study and in two years your mom will be visiting you at Yale, or wherever."

Adam shrugged, but at least he didn't disagree. It was a start. I was still surprised that Adam was so insecure about all this. It was a little weird to reconcile that big, bravado-fueled jock I thought I'd known for all those years with this introspective, caring guy I was discovering him to be. I was really glad he had finally revealed himself to me, and not just in the naked-in-my-bed kind of way. I realized that, somewhere along the line, I had started to care for Adam.

It was a weird thought.

"What about you?" Adam asked. "What do you want to do when you graduate? What's your dream?"

"Oh, something small. Ruler of the World. Batman. That kind of thing."

Adam laughed. "I'm serious. I want to know."

"My dream? Like, that thing you'll probably never do, maybe even never try for, but sometimes you just sit and fantasize about?"

"Yeah."

"I don't know. Nothing."

"Oh come on! You obviously have something in mind."

I hesitated. My dreams were, well, personal.

"Well, sometimes, when I think about my future—and obviously this would probably never happen—but sometimes I dream about running away to some monastery at the top of a mountain or something, and spending the rest of my life singing hymns, like some kind of Gregorian monk."

"Weird haircut and everything?"

"Weird haircut, scratchy brown robe, vow of silence, all of it. I picture a huge Gothic cathedral, silent but for the reverberations, the dying echoes of the last hymn. Surrounded by giant stained glass windows, which are always lit by epic sunsets in my imagination, by the way. I'd spend my days singing and reading—they might frown on all the sci-fi, but I'm sure I could work something out—and doing good deeds, and polishing stained glass windows. Really, the fantasies are, like, seventy percent stained glass window themed."

"I didn't know you were very religious."

"Oh, I'm not, really. I mean, I believe in God. Jesus is pretty cool, though I don't really care whether he really was the son of God or not. The story is powerful enough on its own. And besides, even if there is no God, no higher power of any kind, that doesn't make the universe one iota less amazing, though maybe a tiny bit more depressing. So if I'm not singing praises to some omnipotent deity, then it's to the marvelous entirety of existence. It doesn't especially matter to me either way."

"Worship the universe, huh?"

"Not worship, exactly. More like appreciate. Rather than just take advantage of. People tend to only wonder how to use all the miracles of existence to make their lives easier, which I guess is important too. But I don't think they do enough of that. Appreciate the world and all the things in it, I mean. So I would kind of like to spend my life doing exactly that."

"Appreciation through song and stained glass windows."

"Exactly."

"I like it."

"Really?"

Adam laughed. "Yeah. Why? Is that surprising?"

I shrugged. "I don't know. I've never really told anyone this before."

"Not even Malachi?" Adam sounded pretty incredulous.

"Especially not Kai. He'd just make fun of me. Rightfully so. It is kind of silly. And not, like, in a malicious way or anything. He'd tease me like he does about everything. With anything else I'd be fine with it, but…."

"But when it's your secret dream, it's different."

"Yeah."

"I get that. But if you do decide to go the Batman route, I can always murder your parents for you. You know, anything to help out."

We laughed, then lay for a while in comfortable silence.

Eventually, Adam said, "What time is it?"

"Nooooooo," I protested.

"I don't think 'no' is a time."

"Asking what time it is inevitably leads to saying 'look at the time! I have to go.' How about we just don't?"

But Adam wasn't going to be dissuaded. He pushed me off him, slipped out of the bed, and padded across the room to where his pants were folded on my desk. He rifled through them and found his phone.

"It's almost three," he said to me, then to himself, "Holy shit, that's a lot of messages."

I still lay in bed, watching him standing there, completely naked, listening to voice mails. There might be better ways to spend Saturday afternoons, but I had a hard time thinking of one. He stood with his head cocked to one side, hand on his hip, lower lip caught distractedly in his teeth. I was getting hard, thinking of the things I'd like to do once I convinced him to come back to bed. But as he listened to the messages, a change started to come over his face. Tension returned to his jaw. His eyes became harder, losing the warmth I had seen when he looked at me. He started to fidget.

Finally, the messages came to an end. He started pulling on his pants, turning away from me. "I should go," he said.

See? I was right. Time-checking always leads to me-leaving. It's an undeniable fact. But it didn't seem appropriate to bring that up again, as much as I wanted to do an I-told-you-so gloat.

Instead, I said, "Who were the messages from?"

"Pete," Adam said, pulling on his shirt. "He left me six messages. He started off crying, saying he was sorry, that he didn't want to become like Dad. Begging me to forgive him. Then he got mad I wasn't answering. Then the apologizing again." He sighed. "I need to go home."

Wordlessly, I slipped out of bed, walked over and grabbed Adam in a hug. At first he stood there, like he was stubbornly resisting the affection. Then he hugged me back, squeezing so tight my ribcage almost split open like a nut.

"Thanks," he whispered in my ear.

"You could, just, not."

"And stay here forever?"

"I mean, if you wanted."

He sighed deeply and broke off the hug. "I can't, as cool as that would be. He's being an ass, but he's family. I can't just leave." He went to the window and opened it. I shivered at the sudden blast of cold air. Adam once again popped the screen out of the window, but stopped short of stepping out. He turned back to me and eyed me from head to toe as though memorizing the sight of my still naked body. I fidgeted a little self-consciously at the scrutiny. Adam stepped back up to me and paused, looking a little nervous. Bashful, almost. He gave me a quick peck on the lips. “Bye,” he said. And he left, popping the screen back in the window from the outside.

CHAPTER EIGHT

THE ASTUTE observer might have noticed by now that I was in a bit of a bind. Less than a month ago, I had been a slightly lonely, though impossibly charming, seventeen-year-old with absolutely no romantic prospects on the horizon and, honestly, I wasn't really looking for any. I certainly wasn't expecting any. But now I found myself with two, equal in appeal and in confusion.

What was I going to do?

If this were any other situation, I could do what I usually did when I needed to figure something out: talk it over with Kai. But for the first time in our friendship, I didn't know if I could. It wasn't like it was right before I came out to Kai, when I had been afraid of what he would say or do, or if our friendship would survive. It was more like this nagging feeling he couldn't help. That he was too involved in the situation. I certainly couldn't talk to Mel about it, not without betraying Kai's trust. It was obvious he didn't want her to know about him and me. In my desperation I even considered asking my parents for advice.

Hey Mom, Dad, I've been fucking Kai. It's not what you think—he's probably still straight. My bully, on the other hand, is suddenly all gay for me. Thoughts? You know, maybe it would be worth it, just to see the look on their faces. But no, there was only one thing that was going to work. Awkward as it might be, Kai was my best friend, and I could trust him to help me figure out how I felt. And hopefully find out more about how he felt.

"You're still coming over tonight, right?" I asked him at the lunch table on Monday. Mel was in line for food, and I had seized the opportunity to talk to Kai alone.

"You bet your ass I am." He waggled his eyebrows at me.

"That's not what I meant," I began, but before I could clarify, Mel joined us at the table.

"What's not what you meant?" she asked. Kai immediately turned his attention to the food on his tray, leaving me to face Mel's inquisitive, arched eyebrows alone.

"Uhhhh... nothing. Kai was just being an asshole." Kai snickered, probably thinking I'd made some kind of innuendo, or at least a pun. Dammit, Mel, I was trying to get Kai's mind *off* sex for a little while.

Mel looked unconvinced, but she didn't press further. "Speaking of assholes," she said.

I turned to see what Mel was talking about. Adam was heading straight toward us. *Because of course* that's what would happen right then. I had sort of hoped I might avoid being in any kind of close quarters with both Adam and Kai, but apparently that was out of the question. As if I needed more proof that God had a sense of humor. A sense of humor apparently influenced by too many sitcoms and practical jokes.

Adam smiled when he saw me look his way, which only made things worse. It made me realize that I too was happy to see him, which set off another round of confusion fireworks. Especially when I compared it to the awkward feeling I still felt around Kai in public.

Adam sat down at our table. For a second I thought Kai's eyes were going to pop out of their sockets. He cleared his throat loudly, but if Adam noticed, he gave no sign. "Hey," Adam said to me, continuing to ignore the strange looks my friends were giving him. "I was thinking, maybe—"

"Why are you sitting here," Kai burst in belligerently. "The jock table is over there. You know, the one with all the other idiots."

Adam gave him a slow, sidelong look. It wasn't hostile or threatening, just a look. Nonetheless Kai shifted his shoulders, uncomfortable with the scrutiny. "Malachi," Adam said, as though musing. "Didn't you shit your pants on a field trip in the fifth grade?"

Mel shrieked with laughter. "I *remember* that!" It had been shortly after she moved here. Kai had been trying to lift large rocks at the state park in some pathetic attempt to impress her.

Kai's face had turned some kind of purple. "What's your point?"

"Oh, nothing." Adam said casually, in between bites of his burger. "Just that maybe you should be nicer to people, especially when they still have certain pictures lying around their house."

"There are *pictures* of that? Oh my *God*, you *have* to bring them!" And just like that, Adam had won Mel over. She and Adam began going back and forth, doing their best to imitate the look on Kai's face that day. Even Kai eventually gave in, did an impression of his ten-year-old self, which caused Mel to dissolve into a fit of helpless laughter at how perfectly he was able to recapture the exact expression, a mix of shock, embarrassment, and the fervent hope that he would wake up from the nightmare his life had suddenly become. All in all, it was fun having Adam around. I started to feel the tension drain from my shoulders. Maybe this wouldn't be a disaster.

Adam looked over at me and smiled his most dazzling smile, dimples and all. Under the table, he reached out and grabbed my hand, twining our fingers where no one could see. My heart caught in my throat at the unexpected gesture of affection. I must have had some kind of look on my face, 'cause Adam's smile grew wider, and he winked at me.

I could get used to this.

AFTER LUNCH, I brought my tray over to the garbage cans to dump my trash. Adam had left a while back to meet up with his friends, and Mel and Kai were still reminiscing about the various embarrassing things we had all done in elementary school. It turned out Mel had quite a trove of stories from her old school too. Though really, they could all be made up, not like we knew the kids she mentioned to check if the stories were true. Hilarious nonetheless.

"Dude, what were you doing sitting at that queer's table today? You switching teams on us?" The voice was Will Davis, one of Adam's most obnoxious friends. It came from around the corner, right outside of the lunchroom in the hall.

It was Adam who responded. "Fuck no! You know I hate that faggot."

"That's not what it looked like to us. Looked like you were having a great time with your new boyfriend and his troupe of drama outcasts…."

As quietly as possible, so they wouldn't notice me, I cleaned off my tray, put it in the bin with the others, and made my way back to my table. I didn't want to hear Will spew his vitriolic bullshit anymore, and I especially didn't want to hear how Adam was going to respond to it. I wasn't mad, honest! It's kind of what I had expected. His friends were assholes, he had always cultivated that faux macho façade, and he was obviously so deep in the closet he'd gotten on a first name basis with the mothballs and forgotten shoes. Besides, by all accounts, it seemed as though he really liked me, and I know firsthand how difficult it can be to come to terms with your sexuality. Even with the supportive friends and family I had, which Adam clearly lacked. So no, not mad.

But, I don't know… I guess there had been some kind of hope. Of what? I wasn't sure exactly. I tried not to let myself feel disappointed, and especially not sad. And I was almost successful, until it was Kai who was smiling, calling to me from across the lunchroom, and I was faced anew with my dilemma—straight guy who is comfortable with liking me, and a gay one who isn't.

I WAS pacing nervously as Kai shut the door to my bedroom. I heard the door click as he locked it, but it didn't register. I was too caught up in my thoughts.

"Listen," I said, finally getting up the courage to begin. "Something pretty big happened, and I kinda need to talk to you—"

Kai cut me off. "Something big is about to happen." With a mischievous grin, he pushed me back onto the bed and got on his knees in front of me. "I've been practicing on a Fudgsicle," he said with a wink.

"No, I'm serious. There's something I need to work out and…." Kai had gotten my pants unbuttoned and pulled them down to my ankles. “Wait, you what?” And just like that, Kai swallowed my dick.

I was about to stop him. But when I opened my mouth with every intention of telling him to stop, Adam’s voice flashed through my mind. *You know I hate that faggot.* There was even a bit of an echo, as though my subconscious were trying for dramatic effect. And my protests died unspoken. Why was I supposed to care about that asshole again? In that moment, I couldn’t remember a single reason.

In my defense, I wasn’t thinking too clearly because—and I feel this bears repeating—Kai was sucking my dick. *Kai* was *sucking my dick!*

So, the only words I managed were moaned. “Fuck yeah.”

My cock came out of Kai’s mouth with an audible pop. “Mmmm,” he said. “Penisy. Strangely not terrible.” He licked my shaft from base to tip. “Kind of prefer the Fudgsicle, though.” He laughed and took me back in his mouth.

It was really happening. With Adam completely out of my mind, I marveled in the moment. Kai was sucking my dick. In all our sexual encounters to date, it was mostly with me on the giving and him on the receiving end, and it never seemed to mean as much to him as it did to me. I’d suck his dick, and he’d give me a halfhearted hand job. I’d get hard simply by looking at him while he tended to giggle at the sight of me. Even when I fucked him, he had been passive and somehow left me feeling as emotionally necessary as a dildo.

But now he was sucking my dick. This wasn’t a hand job between buddies; this was something more. And if Kai wanted something more from me, to be more than just friends….

Movement from the corner of my eye caught my attention. I turned my head, saw someone standing outside the window. It was Adam. He was staring at me, at my hard dick, at Kai. His face was rage. No, his face was pain. No, his face was gone.

I stared at the empty window, a conflicting tumult of emotions raging inside of me. “What’s wrong? Am I that bad?” Kai was looking up at me with a sardonic grin, lazily stroking my cock with his hand.

Suddenly, the full import of everything that had happened hit me. Of what exactly we had been doing. There was something I had to know. "Stand up." Kai's eyebrows furrowed at the emotion in my voice, but he did what I said. "Take off your clothes."

"Oooo, feisty, are we?" He pulled his shirt over his head and dropped his pants with an excited quickness. His cock was soft, I couldn't help but notice; I always got hard from giving him a blow job.

"Shut up," I said. I grabbed him, thrust our bodies together, and kissed him hard.

I was panting when I eventually pulled away. Kai had his signature dopey grin on his face. "What did you feel?" I asked him.

"A lot of tongue," Kai quipped.

"Fuck."

Kai's eyebrows furrowed. "What? Not funny?"

"I felt fire, burning in my gut and spreading outward. I felt electricity on every inch of my skin that touched yours. I felt...." Things I had felt with Adam, only he had felt them as well. And now that was ruined too.

I realized I had been yelling. I brought my voice back under control. "I'm falling in love with you, and you will never reciprocate." I grabbed his clothes from off the floor and threw them at him. "You need to go. Now. And we can't hang out for a while."

"But I...." I could see him struggling to be understanding. "Okay," he said finally. He put on his clothes and opened my door. He paused outside in the hall. "Earlier, you said there was something you needed to talk to me about...?"

I couldn't have kept the bite out of my voice if I had tried. And I didn't try. "It's a little late now to start caring about my feelings, don't you think?" I slammed the door in his face, but not before I saw the look of hurt painted there.

For what seemed a very long while, I leaned against the door, listening to Kai in the hall beyond, just standing there. I was waiting, though I had no idea for what. I wasn't dumb enough to expect him to bang on the door, protesting his love, and take me in his arms to my bed. Or maybe I really was that stupid. Eventually I heard Kai's steps retreating down the hall and the sound of the front door slamming.

I slid down the door until I was sitting on the floor. I wondered distantly if I should be crying. Instead, I stared out my window, thinking not of the pain I was in, but rather the pain I had caused.

CHAPTER NINE

SCHOOL BECAME an exercise in misery after that. Of course there would be no explaining anything to Mel. Kai was still my best friend. I needed space to sort my feelings out, and I wasn't about to go sharing secrets that weren't entirely mine. Luckily, in first period math, I showed up late enough that the only available desk was on the opposite side of the room from Mel and Kai. Unfortunately, there was no such luck in biology. The second I stepped in the door, Kai looked at me expectantly and Mel waved. She had no reason yet to suspect anything was amiss. Well, she would in about two seconds.

The only other table with open seats was one populated almost exclusively by cheerleaders. I stepped up to them and asked if I could sit there, ignoring the sight of Mel across the room, eyebrows climbing straight off her forehead.

It was Charlotte who responded. "Sure!" she said with her usual unrestrained enthusiasm and cheerfulness. Charlotte was the undeniable queen of the cheer squad, and James P. Hogan's girlfriend to boot. Which I always wanted to hate her for, but I couldn't 'cause she was just as nice as James P. Hogan himself, and they were obviously all perfect and meant to be and shit. Unfortunately.

So I sat down, trying not to look as hopelessly out of place as I felt. From the corner of my eye, I saw Mel glaring at Kai, her mouth moving rapidly—an obvious interrogation. Kai looked sullen. I felt a pang of regret but angrily pushed it aside. It was his fault all this was happening. He started it, not me, and didn't even pause to think how it might affect me. Affect us.

With a start I realized that the cheer diva sitting next to me was staring, eyes narrowed.

"You're a gay, right?" Her name was Tiffany, I was pretty sure.

I had no idea how to respond. Most of the rest of the girls had dropped their conversations to scrutinize me as well. I looked to Charlotte for help, but she was jotting something down in her notebook, apparently oblivious to my plight.

"Um, yes?"

"Oh. My. God," she squealed, along with the rest of my impromptu audience. "It's a dream come true! Quick, tell Amanda what a skank she looks in that top."

The particularly busty blond across the table scoffed in indignation. "Oh, bitch, you did *not* just say that!"

"Who do you think is the hottest guy in school?" another girl asked.

"Um…." I wasn't about to tell the truth. Charlotte was paying attention now, drawn in by the squealing chorus. Luckily I was saved from answering when Tiffany made a fashion magazine materialize seemingly out of nowhere and began asking my opinion on practically every shoe in there. And no small amount of dresses either.

AS SOON as the bell rang, announcing the end of class, I rushed out of the room. That was another advantage to sitting at the cheerleaders' table: it was right next to the door. I could get out before Mel or Kai had the chance to catch up with me.

"Hey, Dylan, wait up."

I flinched. There went my hasty exit. But at least it wasn't Mel's voice. Instead it was Charlotte, which was a huge surprise. I hadn't realized she even knew my name.

"Sorry about Tiffany and all them," she said, falling in beside me. "Their hearts are in the right place, I promise. They have always wanted a GBFF." She saw the look on my face and clarified. "A gay best friend forever."

"Yeah, I figured. I just had no idea there was a demand."

"Well, you are the only gay guy at school." She gave me a knowing, sidelong look. "At least, the only one who has come out."

That was exactly the kind of thing I did *not* want to be talking about right now. So I changed the subject back to this whole "GBFF" thing. "Well, they'll probably just end up being disappointed. Don't know how well I'll meet their expectations. I guess I could talk about boys with the best of them, but I doubt I'll do that well in the fashion department."

"I don't know. You gave some pretty good advice back there. You've got good instincts."

"Oh goodie," I said sarcastically. "I guess I really am gay, after all."

Charlotte laughed. "Gays and girls. We're only as good as the clothes we wear. Sure feels that way sometimes, doesn't it?"

"Not to mention all the pressure to act a certain way."

"Yeah, but that's everybody, just with different expectations, different standards of normal. Hey, you have English next, right? With James?"

I was taken aback. "How did you know?"

"Oh, James talks about you all the time. Says you're the funniest kid he's met, and definitely one of the smartest."

Wow. I had no idea James P. Hogan ever even thought about me, much less talked about me. If it were any other day, I think I might have swooned.

"Anyway," Charlotte continued. "Why don't I walk with you to class? I have math right down the hall."

This was practically a godsend. Walking with Charlotte was the perfect excuse I needed to avoid running into Mel in the halls. As probably the most popular girl in school, she was almost guaranteed a posse of followers I could utilize to hide from the best friends I didn't quite know how to face today.

I didn't run into Adam that day until lunch. I once again sought refuge with the cheerleaders. Tiffany, in particular, seemed delighted to have me there, absolutely positive that I had some kind of magic gayness I could impart to her. I didn't mind too much. Besides, the cheerleader table was right next to the jock table. I knew Adam would show up eventually. I'd just have to wait.

But when he walked up, saw me there sitting with the cheerleaders, I realized I had no idea what to say. All I could manage was a lame "Hey, Adam." He only looked at me for a moment before he sat down, deliberately turning his back on me.

I stared at his back. I had to say something, to apologize, explain what had happened, something. But seriously, what could I say, with everybody there to overhear? God, all this secrecy I'd suddenly found myself saddled with was killing me. I needed my space from Kai, I couldn't talk to Mel, Adam wouldn't talk to me.... It was all infuriating.

"OMG," Tiffany whispered in my ear, though she was loud enough to be heard by half the lunchroom. "Isn't Adam the hottest guy in school?"

It was odd. James P. Hogan was sitting right there, right next to Adam, and yet I found myself agreeing with Tiffany. "Yeah," I said. "The hottest." I saw Adam's back stiffen. He'd obviously heard me, but he didn't turn around, didn't say anything.

After lunch, I tried to catch up to Adam, hoping to get a chance to talk to him alone, if only for a minute. But he ignored me calling his name. When I finally got close enough to him, Will, his very homophobic friend, turned to confront me.

"What the fuck do you want, fag boy?"

I looked to Adam for support. He only stared back at me with dead eyes, turned, and walked away.

"Fuck off, Will," I said, trying to get past him to catch up with Adam. But Will sidestepped, blocking my path.

"You gonna do something about it, fairy?"

I'd never really contemplated punching anyone before. At least not seriously. I'd always been shorter and thinner than most boys, and my instincts toward self-preservation tended to ward off the thoughts of violence. But in that instant, I came within a millimeter of punching Will right in the face.

"That's what I thought," Will muttered smugly and walked off, leaving me standing there, wishing I had punched him. At least it would have wiped that smug look off his face.

OVER A week of that went by. I didn't go to drama club at all, for fear of facing Mel's questions, though I did send her a "sorry, Kai and I are fighting" text. She never responded. Well, I guess that's another relationship I'll have to repair eventually. I'll add it to the list.

I kept sitting with Charlotte and Tiffany and the rest of the cheerleaders during biology and lunch. Actually, that was the best part of this whole experience. I found myself indulging more and more of my feminine side, what with the constant talk of fashion, the liberal use of the words "bitch" and "gurrrrl," the delight in the daily drama of high school life, slumber parties with makeovers, and boy talk. It was strangely liberating. I consider myself to be a pretty masculine guy. I try not to cry, get strangely defensive about lifting heavy things, pretend I'm not feeling half the emotions I really am, say things like "dude" and "bro," watch tons of action movies, all that fun stuff. But hanging out with these girliest of girls drew out parts of me I'd never explored, hadn't really even known were there. It was the one bright spot, if for no other reason than it introduced me to the wonderful world that is chick flicks.

Kai and I still hadn't spoken, which I thought was for the best. I wanted to be able to look at him without the sight of his cock being the first thing to leap into my mind. Sometimes I worried that it wasn't him I missed, but rather the sex. For a few weeks there, we didn't really do anything outside of that. School was awkward, we barely talked, we were just naked all the time. I hoped that wasn't the case. So in order to be certain, I was going to have to wait until I could look at him without my stomach twisting into knots and my mouth running dry.

Adam got really good at avoiding me. After the first few days of trying to talk to him, only to get the cold shoulder, I guess he must have started taking roundabout ways to class, 'cause I never saw him in the halls. Except for once on Thursday, when he promptly turned right around and went back the way he'd come before getting within forty feet of me. I don't know what he did for lunch, 'cause I stopped seeing him in the lunchroom. I know some kids ate in the orchestra room or the band room, but Adam didn't play an instrument. Maybe the jocks did something similar with the locker room or the gym. I thought about asking James P. Hogan—for whatever reason, I no longer got quite so tongue-tied around him—but I figured it would seem too weird. Wherever Adam was, I could never find him. I was beginning to doubt I'd ever get him to even talk to me, much less forgive me. What I needed was to somehow get him alone, for only five minutes. I felt confident that, when he was not surrounded by hundreds of our peers, he might actually give me a chance to explain myself. Finally, the next Friday, I got my chance.

I had forgotten my textbook in Spanish class, so I headed over to the language hallway to pick it up during lunch. The hallway was empty; kids were either at lunch or in classes. When I left the Spanish classroom, I saw Adam walking down the hall, just a few feet away. He hadn't noticed me step out the door. This was the perfect opportunity to talk to him; no one was around and I was practically close enough to touch him. I ran to catch up.

"Adam, wait," I said, grabbing his arm. "Please, can we talk?"

"What the fuck could you possibly want to say," he replied through clenched teeth. "Leave me alone and go back to your stupid boyfriend."

Okay, so, not the best start, but at least he was talking to me. "It's not what you think. Kai is straight."

Adam's face twisted with anger. "Is that supposed to make me feel better?" he demanded, shoving me up against the locker, fists bunched up in my shirt. Unshed tears were gathering in his eyes. "Is it? You can't land the Jewish faggot of your dreams so you'll settle for me?"

The pressure Adam was exerting on my chest was kind of painful, but I didn't care. I was just happy he was actually talking to me again, and it felt good to have him touching me, even like this. Besides, I kinda think maybe I deserved it. I grabbed his wrists so he wouldn't let go.

"No, it's not like that. I swear."

"Oh yeah? Well, what is it like?"

Well, here we go. I thought. I still had no idea how to explain myself, but I finally had him listening so I'd better dive right in. But before I could even begin, an all too familiar voice broke in.

"Now, now, boys. I'm getting pretty tired of finding you two like this." Mr. Cortez stood there, arms folded, looking stern.

Adam immediately let go of me and pulled his arms out of my grip with barely any effort. He took off down the hall, and with him went all my hopes of reconciliation. Every last scrap of self-control I had snapped. All the frustration and anger that had been slowly building for over a week burst forth.

"God *damn* it, you fucking *idiot*! Do you have any idea what you just did? That was the first time I have gotten him to talk to me in fucking *weeks*, but you just had to butt in and 'rescue' me, 'cause that is apparently the only thing that validates your worthless existence."

Mr. Cortez took a step backward under the force of my anger. At that moment I realized exactly what I'd done, and how stupid it was.

"I mean… no, fuck it, that's exactly what I mean. Don't worry, I'll just show myself to Mr. Hayes's office."

CHAPTER TEN

DINNER THAT night was a strange affair. I had kind of figured that after getting a phone call from the principal explaining exactly what I had done and that I was suspended for the next week, there might be some degree of, I don't know, punishment perhaps? At the very least, some scolding, maybe a withheld dessert. The kind of things parents are supposed to do, you know? Instead, dinner was painfully, awkwardly normal. Cheery even.

Neither of my parents made any mention of my suspension. They only talked about work, like usual. Meanwhile, I was practically jumping at every loud sound, expecting the fire and brimstone parents are supposed to rain down in this situation. It only got worse the longer it took to come.

But dinner ended and still no yelling or recrimination. I leaped to do the dishes, hoping to lessen the punishment that obviously *had* to be coming. Only it never came. My parents turned on the TV in the living room like it was a completely normal Friday. Finally I slunk back to my room.

I wasn't in there for more than a minute when Dad knocked on the door. *Here it comes*, I thought, *the yelling, scolding, grounding.* I didn't look up when Dad opened the door. I kept my eyes firmly fixed on the floor, looking out of the corner of my eye at Dad's feet standing in the doorway.

"You ready to talk about it?"

He didn't sound angry at all. I was incredulous. "What?" I asked, looking up. Dad was leaning against the doorframe, arms crossed.

"Everything that's been going on. Ready to talk about it yet?"

"That's it?" I asked. Dad raised an eyebrow. "I mean, no yelling, no punishment? I was suspended. Aren't you mad?"

Dad shrugged.

"We're a little disappointed, your mother and I. Well, more me. Your mother finds this whole thing kind of funny, especially making you squirm all throughout dinner." My jaw was resting on the floor, I was certain. Dad laughed at the look on my face. "Listen, Dylan, you're a good kid. We know that. We also know that you haven't been yourself lately. I'm going to take a wild guess and say it had something to do with Mr. Mysterious from a few weeks ago, not to mention the complete lack of Kai eating us out of house and home lately and this constant moping in your room." Wow. I was a little stunned at how observant my parents were. Here I was thinking I had been acting completely normal, and they could see right through me the entire time. "So, no. I'm not mad. Besides, what would I do, ground you to your room? You already never leave this place. Kind of sad, really."

I laughed. "Thanks. You really know how to cheer a guy up."

"Glad I could help. You want to come sit with your mother and me? There's a Hitchcock marathon on tonight."

"Nah, I think I'm just gonna go to bed."

"Alright, son. Sleep tight." He started to pull the door shut, but paused with it open a crack. "And seriously, Dylan, if you ever need to talk, we're right here. We may be old, but we can probably understand what you're going through a little better than you think."

"Thanks, Dad. I will."

WHEN MEL finally burst through my cocoon of self-pity, I had barely left my room for four days. She practically beat down my door, dragged me from the protective warmth of my blankets, literally kicking and screaming, with one hand grabbing my wrist, the other with a fistful of hair, and forced me to take my first shower all week, ignoring my protestations the entire way. She shoved me in the bathtub, still completely clothed, and turned on the water, drenching me.

"I assume you can do the rest?"

I sputtered under the cold water, still trying to come to terms with what was happening. Seconds ago I had been so warm and cozy! But Mel didn't wait for an answer. She left, slammed the bathroom door behind her. So I peeled off my soaked pajama bottoms, turned up the temperature of the water, and did as I was told.

It actually felt really good to get clean. There's a certain trajectory to ignoring all aspects of your personal hygiene. First, you feel all gross. Sweaty, greasy, dirty, all of it. But by the end of day two, that passes, and this slimy swamp monster, as you have suddenly found yourself, becomes the new normal. Before long, you begin to resent the very idea of getting clean, and shedding this second skin you've so carefully developed, because it might mean you have to go back to being who you were, and you're in no way ready to do that.

But as the swamp monster crumbled away, and I felt more and more like a person again, everything seemed a little better. Sure, my life had suddenly fallen into shambles. Adam would probably never talk to me again, and I don't know when I'll be able to face Kai, if ever. But now that I was clean, I felt like I could face the world again.

Well, almost.

When I got back to my room, towel wrapped around my waist, I found that Mel had made herself busy. She'd cleaned up the days' worth of dishes I'd left piled on my floor, changed the sheets on my bed, opened the shades on my windows. She had even laid out clean clothes on my bed for me to get dressed.

"I knew my best friend was hiding somewhere under all that grease and body odor," Mel quipped as I walked in. She was sitting at my desk, idly paging through one of my books. She turned her back to me, giving me some privacy to change.

"How did you get in?" I asked as I pulled on my clothes.

"Your mom texted me. Said it was about time someone pulled you out of your funk." She gestured at my suddenly tidied room "What, did you think *I* did all this for you? I mean, I like you, but come on."

"Oh." I hadn't even realized my mom was home, though that might have had something to do with my adamant refusal to let them near me for the past few days. "Okay, I'm dressed." I dropped back down onto my bed, but refrained from crawling under the covers. To be honest, I was a little afraid of what Mel might try next, if she thought I was about to undo all her hard work dragging me out in the first place.

Mel closed the book and turned the chair to face me. "Good. Now talk."

I avoided her eyes. "About what?" I asked with exaggerated innocence.

"Fine. Be that way. I'll just have to make a few guesses about what has been going on lately." Yeah, right. Like she could possibly…. "First, you and Malachi have been getting sexy, to some degree or other, until about three weeks ago when I'm going to say it was you who called it off. Possibly because Adam found out and got jealous. How am I doing so far?"

Okay, what was it about me that everyone could apparently see completely through? Do I have any secrets at all? Am I actually an open book for anyone to read at their leisure?

"I take it from the look on your face I was pretty close. So let's see, you stopped talking to me because you're an idiot, you've been trying to get Adam to talk to you at school 'cause, again, you're an idiot, and went ahead and got yourself suspended. Like an idiot."

"How did you know?"

Mel muttered "idiot" under her breath. "Dylan, I pay attention. I know you only got into drama club because you went through an 'am I gay enough' phase and decided you needed to do a musical, and Malachi followed you like the little lost puppy he is. But theater is what I actually want to do with my life. I pay attention to people, how they behave, why they behave that way. So when you and Kai started acting like you had this giant secret no one could ever find out while simultaneously being very careful not to accidentally touch in public, ever, it wasn't much of a mental workout to figure out what was going on. And then there was the sudden transformation of Adam, from bully to buddy, not to mention the covert looks he kept casting your way when he thought you weren't looking. Plus there was the time—"

"Okay, okay! I get it!"

"Good. Now that we've established that you can't hide anything from me, ever, why don't you actually tell me what's been going on? At the very least you'll feel better."

"I don't know about that."

"Yeah, 'cause keeping it in has been working so well."

I sighed. She was right, of course. "Okay, fine. So, um, remember that day I got punched in the face?" She nodded. "Well, that's when Adam and I started to be… well, friends, I guess. Which made Kai all kinds of jealous…."

I recounted the entire story, right up to my brief interaction with Adam before I got suspended. Mel listened quietly to the whole story, occasionally asking a question or two. I told her everything. Well, maybe I glossed over a little bit of the sexy-time details, but that didn't seem entirely appropriate. When I finally finished, over an hour later, she sat there silently for a minute, absorbing.

"So, what are you going to do?" she finally asked.

"What can I do? I mean, I can't talk to him. It's still too weird. I know he's my best friend, but that's exactly why I have to…."

"Malachi's fine where he is. He knows you need space. I meant about Adam."

"Oh." I bit my lip, thinking. "I don't know. He wouldn't even talk to me."

"Did you apologize?"

"Of course I… wait, no. I just said that he didn't understand." Suddenly I got really angry. "And why should I apologize? It's not like I did anything wrong! Kai and I had been fooling around for weeks before Adam snuck into my bedroom. What's more, Adam has spent his whole life trying to make mine miserable. Am I supposed to just magically forgive him for all of that, be whatever it is he wants me to be? Fuck that. All we did was fool around one night. What did he want, to be my boyfriend? No, he wanted me to be his secret fling, to use at his leisure. So why should I apologize? It's not like I promised anything anyway." My excuses were starting to sound hollow even to my ears.

Mel was giving me a very flat look. "Okay. I'm going to ignore, like, half of the idiocy you just spouted. So I'll skip right to the point. You don't apologize to people because they are right and you aren't. You apologize to people because you hurt them. Whether you meant to or not. Regardless of whether you think you did anything wrong. That's called respecting other people's feelings, AKA not being a douchebag. No wonder you couldn't get Adam to talk to you. What did you think, that you'd only have to say 'it didn't count 'cause he's, like, ninety percent straight' and Adam would heave a sigh of relief and you two could skip off into the sunset?"

"That kind of is what I said."

"Did it work?" Mel asked. I shook my head. "Look," she continued, "I'm not saying you *have* to apologize to Adam. Honestly, you sort of had a point. He has been your bully forever. But if that's your tactic, that you don't care because he used to be mean, you really should think twice about moping around your room all day. One might think you actually do care. A lot. A casual observer might, for example, come to the conclusion that you're lying to yourself, because you don't want to swallow your pride, admit you fucked up, pun intended, and take some responsibility for your actions."

"Okay, fine. Let's say I do that. Then what?"

"What do you mean?"

"What I mean is, what happens next? Do I go back to being a dirty little secret? I mean, what even *am* I to Adam? It's not like he'll come out for me. He won't even be *friends* with me. You've seen how he acts around Will Davis, even since we've started hanging out. Wouldn't I have just been better off sticking with Kai? At least with him I know where I stand."

"Listen, you need to get Malachi out of your mind. One day he'll find happiness in some bisexual polyamorous relationship, but until then he's just going to chase all the sexual satisfaction he can find. Is that really what you want to get involved in?" It wasn't. I want the sappy, "run off into the sunset" kind of romance, and she knew that perfectly well. "I know it's not what *I* want. Why do you think I've resisted his numerous advances? You're right. Maybe Adam won't come out for you. Maybe all you'll ever be is his shameful secret. The real question is, are you willing to take that risk?"

"I don't know." I looked over at Mel, realized I was scared. "What if he doesn't actually like me? What if I'm only convenient—the only gay guy he knows?"

Mel shrugged. "You know him better than I. But really, only he can answer that question. Now would you look at the time! I really must be going."

"You're leaving?" I asked, "Just like that?"

She paused at the door to my room. "Listen, some of us weren't suspended for heartbreak histrionics, and so have school in the morning. Think about what I said, okay? In the meantime, maybe leave your room a bit."

THE NEXT day, I took Mel's advice. I made it out of my room, at least as far as the kitchen, and I thought about what she said. She was definitely right about Kai, but I really already knew that. It's just that throughout my life he's always been a point of such certainty. With Adam, there was nothing but uncertainty. It made sense that I kept coming back to feeling like I needed to choose between the two, between the guy I'd always wanted and the guy I never expected.

And hey, maybe the answer is neither of them. Maybe a third guy will waltz along who is *both* something I always wanted and never expected. Voilà, problem solved.

The doorbell rang as if in answer to my thoughts. When I opened the door, I found standing on my front step none other than James P. Hogan, wearing his letterman jacket and the sweatpants he always had on after he finished football practice or a workout, the ones that always gave tantalizing hints of what lay beneath that bulge at the crotch.

"Holy shit, I wasn't being serious," I said without thinking.

James P. Hogan raised an eyebrow, giving me his trademarked amused smirk.

"Um, what? I mean, hi, James." I had to stop myself from adding the "P. Hogan." I had already made enough of a fool of myself, and he had only been here for less than a minute. "What's up?"

"I bring the gift of knowledge." His eyes twinkled. He pulled a stack of papers out of his bag. "By which I mean a week's worth of homework."

"For me? You shouldn't have." James laughed at the sarcasm in my voice. "Um, you wanna come in?"

"Sure," he said, stepping inside. He gestured at me with the papers. "The English work is pretty self-explanatory. Mr. Cortez is on another one of his SAT-prep binges, so it's mostly analogies. The math looks like it's just some simple sine/cosine nonsense. I can explain all that if you want. Your bio homework is all drawing molecules. I brought Charlotte's answers if you wanted to check your work. I assumed choir doesn't have any homework, but I guess you could sing some scales if you wanted. I never took econ so you're on your own there." He dropped the homework on the kitchen table and sat down.

"Wait, you got *all* of my homework?" I asked, sitting across from him. "We only have English together."

He shrugged. "Mr. Cortez asked if someone could bring you the homework, and since you and Charlotte have been hanging out so much lately, I knew where you lived, so I volunteered. Figured while I was at it, I could stop at all your other classes."

"But how did you even know what my classes were?" I had no idea what classes anyone took, except for Melanie and Kai.

Another shrug. "I pay attention." He looked out the window for a second before casually dropping, "Adam misses you."

I tried to sound nonchalant. "Oh. I—what?" I wasn't very successful. "I mean, he said that?"

James P. Hogan looked back at me. "Not in so many words. He's gotten really withdrawn, ignores everybody, his friends included. A week ago he was so mad all the time that even Coach noticed it. Now, nothing."

"And you think that's because of me?"

"Listen, I don't mean to overstep my bounds or whatever. God knows I've never really understood the strange friendship you two have…."

"Friendship? That's not exactly the word I'd use."

James P. Hogan raised an eyebrow. "Really? Then what would you use? I have never met any two people who take as much pleasure in 'fighting' as you and he, and with such a complete lack of any actual malice. Plus, you two hang out all the time."

"That was only recently we started hanging out."

"Still." I was stunned. Did everyone think Adam and I had been friends this whole time? Or only James P. Hogan? "Look, all I'm saying is I think you should talk to him."

We lapsed into silence for a minute.

"You really think we've been friends this whole time?" I finally asked.

"You really didn't?"

I shrugged. "I always figured we were worst enemies. I mean, he was always so mean to me."

"You guys always seemed to enjoy yourselves."

"Recently, maybe. Sure. But it hasn't always been that way. In elementary school he was downright cruel. I don't even know how many times he made me cry."

James started rifling through the pages of my homework, continuing without looking at me. "You know in elementary school, I used to be really mean to Charlotte. It wasn't 'cause I hated her. Quite the opposite actually. I would pinch her, call her names, show her frogs to make her scream…."

"Adam used to shove the frogs down my pants."

"There you go. He was a little more direct than I was."

"But that's different. You had a crush on Charlotte." James gave me a flat look. A look that said "I think we both know it isn't so different."

"Oh. How did you know?"

"Dude. Come on."

CHAPTER ELEVEN

NIGHT WAS falling, and the breeze off the lake was making me chilly. November had kind of snuck up on me, and I had foolishly neglected to wear anything warmer than a sweatshirt. After James left, I made my dad drive me out to Adam's lakeside spot. I'd been there enough times to remember the way. Dad, luckily, hadn't asked why I suddenly needed to go out into the middle of nowhere, much less be left there alone. I don't know what I would have told him. That had been hours ago, and Adam still hadn't shown up. It was beginning to look like I'd have to call and ask Dad to pick me up.

Headlights shone through the trees. I clutched my knees to my chest and kept my eyes on the lake. The car came to a stop, headlights shining right on me. A second later I heard the car start to pull away, stop, pull back in. A minute passed. I fought the urge to look his way. If Adam was going to talk to me, he would. Jumping up and running at the car would probably only scare him away. After what seemed like an eternity, the headlights went out, the car turned off, and I heard the car door open and Adam get out.

I counted the steps Adam took to me. Twenty-three. I still didn't look his way. Maybe I was afraid he would change his mind, think I was being too insistent or something, get back in his car, and I'd lose my chance to ever make things up to him. Or that this wasn't even Adam and I was, like, two seconds away from getting murdered. But after those twenty-three steps, he stopped, right beside where I sat. Out of the corner of my eye, I could see his legs. They looked like Adam legs. I decided I probably wasn't going to be murdered.

Instead I would just have to convince Adam to forgive me. Talking to Mel and James convinced me I had to try. I only wish I had any idea how. So I started simple.

"I'm sorry."

Waves lapped loudly on the shore of the lake. Once. Twice. Three times. "Yeah," Adam finally responded.

Okay, so far so good. There was no yelling, no running away. No punches in the jaw, which, I reminded myself, had actually been a possibility. Only now I had no idea where to go. Thousands of things kept popping into my mind, but sitting there, they all seemed merely excuses.

Adam broke the silence. "Would you rather we talked in my car? It's warmer in there."

"What?"

"You're shaking."

I was, I realized. Funny, how you can be so focused you don't even notice your own body. "Oh. That's not 'cause I'm cold. That happens sometimes when I'm afraid. The first time it happened was when I came out to Kai. I was afraid he wouldn't be my friend anymore." Adam shuffled his feet at the mention of Kai, and I berated myself for bringing him up now. When Adam spoke, he sounded a little angry.

"Yeah? Well, what do you have to be scared of now?"

I took a deep breath, steeling myself. "Of losing you."

The shaking stopped, the world fell silent. This had happened the last time too, once I had worked up the courage to say what I was afraid of, the physical manifestation of that fear vanished, and I was left alone in interminable waiting for the nightmare to come true.

Adam sighed. He sat down next to me, put his arm around my shoulder and pulled me against him. My head fell on his shoulder. "I mean, I haven't completely decided yet, but I don't think that's going to happen."

I giggled. Hey, relief does funny things to people. "So, you forgive me?"

"The way I figure it, you were nice to me once when I didn't deserve it, so now it's my turn to return the favor."

"I want you to know that I haven't spoken to Kai since… you know."

"That's stupid. He's your best friend. Bros before hos… or whatever saying applies in this situation." He was making an effort to sound lighthearted, but I could hear the strain in his voice, feel the tension in his body.

"I needed to make things right with you first."

"Thanks," he said. The strain was mostly gone from his voice, but I didn't feel him relax at all. "How long?"

He didn't say what, but I knew he was talking about me and Kai fooling around. "A few weeks."

"But he's not gay?"

I shook my head. "We were horny, and fooling around was fun."

"But if he were…."

"If he were gay, we would probably have been in a committed relationship since puberty."

"So I really am just second best."

Fuck. I should have been more careful about what I said. "If it makes you feel better, you're both below James P. Hogan." Oh shit, seriously? That was the best I could come up with?

To my surprise, Adam laughed. "Well, that goes without saying. James is by far the hottest guy in school."

"Right? He's been number one on my list for *years*. And you get to see him in the locker room every day! If anyone should be jealous here, it's me."

"Well, I never fucked James."

So much for levity. I fell silent. He was right, after all.

"So, if James is your number one, where do I fall on that list?" Adam said.

"Number three. Recently promoted, in fact."

"I see. And Kai is number two."

"What? No. Number two has always been Sanjay Patel."

"That nerdy Indian kid?"

"He had eyes like starlight."

"He moved away in the eighth grade."

"And Oak Lake still echoes with the memory of him."

We laughed. I started to hope maybe the hard part was over. But Adam wasn't quite finished.

"So where is Malachi on that list?"

I lifted my head to look at Adam. He kept staring forward, not meeting my eyes. "Four."

"And you said I was recently promoted."

"Mmhmm."

"From?"

"Four."

"Let me guess, that changed when I caught you with Malachi and you decided to settle for me."

"No. It was when I saw you naked, and then you kissed me. Actually, when you kissed me you shot up to number one. It took a long while for me to come to my senses and put James back in his rightful place." I expected at least a chuckle on that one, but I didn't get anything. I spun around until I was sitting face to face with Adam. "You keep saying that I'm settling for you, and I don't know what to say to make you realize that isn't true. Yeah, if Kai were gay we'd be dating. What did you expect? That I'd be secretly pining after you? You were my *bully*, Adam. Sure, the last, like, five years it's almost been friendly abuse between us, but I only realized I didn't hate you this year. Imagine how much of a shock it was to find out that you've actually had a crush on me for who knows how long—"

"Fifth grade."

"Did you expect… wait, fifth grade? Really?" He nodded. "Fifth grade was the worst. You made me cry almost every day."

His face fell. "I'm sorry. I didn't know you cried. I just…."

"Yeah. No, I get it. Scared of your sexuality. I've been there. Don't feel bad, all that's behind us. I'm sorry I brought it up. I only wanted to point out how through all of that, Kai was there for me and you weren't."

His face fell even further, which I hadn't thought possible. "You're right. It makes sense you'd choose him over me."

"No, goddamn it!" I'd had it. Out of frustration, I punched him in the leg. His head snapped up, a look of surprise on his face. "I'm saying that even with all that, I'm choosing you, you fucking idiot!

I'm not trying to tell you why you're second best, I'm trying to tell you why it took me so long to realize…."

"Realize what?"

It was my turn to avoid his gaze. "You know. Feelings and stuff."

I sneaked a peek. He was smiling at me. So I kept going. "I've opened up to you like I haven't opened up to him. Even in the short time we haven't been at each other's throats. When that thing with Kai happened, it was like a dream come true. So much so that I ignored all the problems with it. And there were many. I felt *used*, Adam. It was almost like a one-night stand, but one that happened over and over. And our friendship suffered because of it. But I ignored it, 'cause I was lonely, and I wanted his dick so bad. But then you came along, made me feel, I don't know. Safe. And warm. It brought us closer, even at school where everyone could see. That night I wanted to talk to Kai, to tell him about you, what had happened. I didn't know what to do. I was feeling so many things. But then he was sucking my dick, and it was *amazing*. I don't know if maybe some cheerleader's gone down on you under the bleachers or something—ew, don't tell me, I don't want to know—but blow jobs are the best. But then I saw you in the window, and it woke me up to just how *wrong* everything was, even if it felt amazing. Oh God, you looked so hurt. I felt so terrible. I'm really, really sorry. I should have stopped him, I should have done something, I should have never even started fucking Kai to begin with. I should have…."

Adam reached up and touched my face, stopping me. He wiped tears I didn't realize I was shedding off my cheeks. He said, "I forgive you. Can you forgive me?"

"For what?"

"For lying to you since the fifth grade. For making you cry. For doing anything except holding you and kissing you."

"Oh. That." I sniffed. "I guess. If I have to."

Adam laughed. "Come on," he said, standing up. "Let's get you home."

"I can't. Being around you makes me too weak in the knees." Adam chuckled. The next thing I knew I was being lifted off the ground and carried toward the car. "Ahhh! I forgot you had muscles." I wrapped my arms around his neck. "That's a lie. I could never forget."

Once we got in the car, however, my confidence evaporated. When he started driving, Adam grew silent. Almost distant. I mean, this wasn't entirely new, driving in the car with him in the past had usually been quiet. But back then we hadn't just made up after weeks of tension. I began to worry that, given a few minutes of silent contemplation, Adam was going to rethink forgiving me. I guess a part of me was being fatalistic, like it couldn't believe the apparent happy ending that seemed to be unfolding here. Something *had* to go wrong, like immediately, right?

I studied his face, trying to see if there was some sign of, I don't know, turmoil or something beneath the surface. But he seemed kind of blank. He didn't appear at all upset, but he didn't exactly seem happy either.

Adam must have noticed my scrutiny, 'cause he looked my way. I quickly looked out the window, feeling my face blush. *Real smooth, there, Dylan.* If Adam thought I was being weird, he didn't say anything.

Oh God, why isn't he saying anything? Maybe he likes driving in silence? Maybe he's waiting for me to say something first? I racked my brain for something to say to break the silence, but I couldn't think of anything that didn't scream "I'm insecure. Please reassure me!" The crippling quiet stretched on.

It didn't help that the ride back to my house wasn't a short one. By the time we made it there, I was practically quivering with worry. He pulled up in front of my driveway.

Well, this was my chance. "Do you want to come in?" I sounded totally nonchalant. Not insecure at all.

"I can't." Adam said, without turning his head. "I have school tomorrow."

"Oh," I said, fighting to keep the disappointment out of my voice. "That's cool!" Oh God, I was being way too cheery. Overcompensating. I need to play it cool. "Then I'll see you whenever. I guess." I got out of the car, feeling several different kinds of awkward. "Um. Bye." I quickly shut the door and hurried up the driveway.

I heard Adam's car door opening behind me. "Wait," Adam called. I turned around but kept my eyes firmly fixed on the ground in front of me. Adam jogged to catch up to me. "I, um," he mumbled. I watched his feet fidget. "I wanted to, uh...." Suddenly he grabbed my head with both hands, lifted my face, and kissed me.

Several minutes later, Adam pulled away. "Do that," he finished. He started walking backward toward his car. "I'll stop by tomorrow. I mean, if that's cool? I don't want to—I mean, if you have plans or anything...." He was clearly flustered. It was cute. His butt bumped into the car, and he jumped in surprise, then laughed sheepishly. "Tomorrow. I'll call." With that, he got in his car and drove away.

I was grinning like a fool. I had been since he kissed me, but I didn't care. I hadn't realized it until that moment, but that kiss was what I had been waiting for. It was the final proof I needed that Adam really had forgiven me. That things were, maybe not back to normal exactly, but at least back on track. I couldn't help the dopey grin. I watched until his car disappeared around the corner before finally turning and heading inside.

Mom and Dad were still up. As I walked into the living room, Dad looked up from where he was sprawled on the couch, one leg over the armrest. The TV was on, but he was facing away from it.

"Oh," he said. "Hey."

Mom was leaning against the wall, paging through an encyclopedia I had never even seen opened in my life. "How was your night?" she asked, without looking up.

The whole scene reeked of staged nonchalance and forced casualness. I was not fooled. "Let me guess. You were both watching through the kitchen window."

My dad said, "No," at the same second my mom said, "Oh, totally." They exchanged a look and moved into normal human positions. Dad sat up. Mom put the encyclopedia back with the other dust-covered volumes and sat next to him.

"Are you going to tell us who this mystery man is yet?" Mom continued.

"You couldn't see?" I asked.

"No! It was too dark."

"Bummer." I said with a wicked grin. "The suspense must be killing you." With that, I went to my room, ignoring my parents' complaints.

CHAPTER TWELVE

THE NEXT morning, Friday, I woke up to a text from an unfamiliar number.

Hey, it's Adam, it read. *Forgot I have practice after school. I'll come over after.*

There was another one, from Mel.

I gave Adam your number. Assuming you two made up. Yay. Now hurry up and talk to Malachi. I'm tired of his moping.

I smiled, trying to imagine Adam asking Mel for my number. He probably would have tried to be supersecretive about it—avoiding his friends and trying to catch Mel alone—and of course he wouldn't say why he wanted it. Not that Mel would have had any doubt in her mind why he wanted it, but I could picture her giving him a hard time, just for fun. It's exactly what I would have done. I wish I could have seen it.

But my good mood quickly evaporated as I thought about the other thing Mel had said in her text. Up to that point, I had managed, with varying degrees of success, to keep Kai out of my mind. But now things were different. Adam and I were back... well, to whatever this thing we had was, so that wasn't a reason to keep putting off talking to Kai. All that was left was the confusing bundle of emotions that were my feelings toward Kai. After that day I'd stopped talking to him, I just shoveled those into some dark recess of my mind and tried my best to ignore them. I realized I was afraid to examine them again.

But was that enough reason to keep pushing away my best friend since, like, forever? And worse, if I was avoiding Kai because I was afraid of falling in love with him, then what did that say about this relationship-type thing I was starting with Adam?

Mel was right. I needed to talk to Kai, put that part of my life finally behind me. I'd just neglect to mention that to Mel. I hated her smug, I'm-always-right look. Just 'cause it was true didn't mean you could gloat.

I pulled out my phone and stared at a blank text. At least half an hour passed. I had typed nothing.

Breakfast, I decided, needed to precede a text of this magnitude. I made pancakes. Cereal, while by far my favorite, would have been made and eaten far too quickly, and since this was clearly a procrastination meal, I needed to get the most bang for my buck. I even made sausages, which, though I was way overfull, I ate all of. Then scrambled eggs, which I ate none of. Then I did all the dishes. Then cleaned the counter. Then took a shower. Then ate those scrambled eggs. Then waited while the dishwasher ran. Put the clean dishes away. Showered again. Realized only when I started shampooing my hair that I had done so already today. Felt foolish. Spent twenty minutes in the shower anyway. Got dressed. Changed my mind, put my pajamas back on. Changed my mind again, got dressed, this time in a different outfit.

By the time I had finally exhausted every little thing I could think of to do, short of deciding to finish a book, or Netflix-marathon a couple of TV shows, over three hours had passed. It was well past noon. I went back to my cell phone and found, to my dismay, that the text was still blank. I had half hoped my phone would have grown impatient and written the text for me. Isn't that what Siri was supposed to be for? Maybe I should....

With a sigh, I made myself stop putting off the inevitable. Not letting myself overthink it anymore, I whipped out a text to the guy I hoped could still be my best friend.

Kai, we should talk. Come over after school?

Two seconds later, my phone buzzed with a reply.

Not until you spell my name right.

Okay, Chi, I sent back.

Dammit, came the response, *now you have ME saying it wrong.*

I laughed despite myself. All the anticipatory tension I'd had suddenly drained away. I texted back, *If there were two of you, we could call you "the Cheese."*

You're the worst. Friendship over. Then, a second later, *See you soon.*

I flopped down on my bed with a relieved sigh. Now I just have to wait—I checked the time—a little over two hours. Shit. I wished I had saved some of those procrastination tasks for now. I'd had enough breakfast that I probably wouldn't be hungry until, like, midnight. Oh well. At least this would give me an opportunity to come up with what I wanted to say.

Maybe I could take a shower….

WHEN KAI eventually arrived, we spent the first ten minutes or so standing on opposite sides of my room, silent, staring at each other. I couldn't help but imagine tumbleweeds rolling across the room between us, like we were two cowboys who had shown up to the noon shootout, each waiting for the other to make the first move. But I figured I would have to start. That seemed fair.

So, finally, I broke the silence.

"Why?"

"Why what." I didn't answer. Instead I stared flatly at him. Expectantly. He sighed. "I thought it would be fun. And it was. I thought you would like it. You clearly did. I did too. I don't really understand what happened."

"Really?" He looked away, shrugged. "Do you have any idea how careful I've always been around you? How careful I've always had to be? I'll take that confused look to mean 'no.' You get naked at the drop of a hat, Kai. I wish that was only a figure of speech, but you literally dropped a hat once and, for some reason, thought it would be funny to hang it on your dick like a coatrack. On the one hand, it's nice you feel that comfortable around me. It's refreshing to have someone not act like I'm going to prey on them or something. But on the other hand, you're very hot, and I very much like dicks. I was always afraid that if I ever saw you naked, I wouldn't be able to think of you as my best friend anymore, but as a really hot guy with a really hot dick that I wanted but could never have. So I always kept my eyes firmly away. Which wasn't always easy. You wanted me to see your dick-hatrack, remember?"

"But you didn't have to—"

"Yes, I did! You were not just some random hot guy. You're my best friend. I already loved you. The only thing that kept me from being *in* love with you was that your dick was happily off limits. That's why casually fooling around was never going to work for me. I wanted more than you could give me. And the worst part was we even stopped being friends, really, while all that was going on."

"What?" Kai looked shocked, angry even at the suggestion.

"You got all awkward around me at school."

"You did too!"

"I was trying not to fall in love with you. What was your excuse? You didn't want Mel to find out?" Kai looked like he was about to argue, but I didn't let him start. "And that's not even the worst part. Things were happening, big things, that I needed my best friend for. Not his dick, but my actual best friend. And you weren't there for me." I found myself fighting back tears. "God, I've always been there for you. When you were all heartbroken that Mel wouldn't go out with you. When your dad died. You were there for me when Adam was bullying me to tears every day, but you couldn't get your mind off sex long enough to be there when he…." I trailed off.

"What? When he what? What did that asshole do now?" Kai looked furious, his hands curled into fists.

"Nothing. Well, I mean, he did some things, but nothing bad." Kai looked completely confused. "You know that night we… the last time we hung out?" Kai nodded. "Well, like two days before that, Adam showed up at my house in the middle of the night and… well, it turns out he's gay too, and he only bullied me so no one would realize how he *actually* felt about me."

"Oh." He paused, clearly trying to come to grips with what he'd heard. "Why didn't you tell me?"

"I tried. You were a little preoccupied. With my dick."

Kai laughed softly. "I guess I was. I'm sorry." He paused. "You're right. I should have been there for you. It must have been hard, having that creep come on to you." Kai's eyes suddenly lit up. "What did you say to him? Did you call him all the names he ever called you? Did you vomit, like, all over his entire body?"

"Actually, kind of the opposite happened."

"He vomited all over you? How did *that* come about?"

"No, I mean we kind of…." I trailed off again. For some reason, I couldn't quite bring myself to tell Kai that Adam and I had slept together.

"You what? You…." He suddenly gasped in realization. "Oh. You mean… you and he…?" I nodded. Kai's eyes grew wide, like a hurt puppy dog's. "You left me for Adam?"

I burst out laughing. I couldn't help it. Kai looked even more hurt. "Really? You're jealous? You are still straight, right?"

"Yeah, it's just… you don't like him better than me, do you?"

"No, of course not. Well, in that *like*-like way, yeah, but he actually *like*-likes me too."

"I guess," Kai said. I could almost swear he was pouting.

"Are you sulking?"

"No. Shut up. I'm just saying… I could too."

I laughed. He was definitely sulking. "Listen, you had your chance."

"But *Adam*?"

"He's actually really nice. He really seems to care about me too."

"Adam."

"Yeah, I know. I was surprised too. Kind of one of the things I wish I could have shared with you back when it was first happening."

Kai gave a sheepish look. "I'm sorry. But you can tell me now! Okay. Start from the beginning. Tell me the whole story."

"Well…." I said, looking at the clock.

Kai sighed. "Let me guess. Adam's coming over soon."

"Well, I don't know about soon, but eventually."

"All right," Kai grumbled. "I guess I can get out of your hair. Let you get ready for Loverboy to show up."

"Speaking of which, you can't tell anyone about Adam. I don't think he'd even like it that I told you."

"I mean, I figured. I'm not an idiot."

"Could have fooled me."

"Hey now." Kai said with a smile. "I'll see you later, then?"

"Yeah."

Throughout our entire conversation, we had maintained our distance, standing on opposite sides of the room from each other. Kai finally breached that gap, walking across the room and grabbing me in a big hug. For a split second I was uncomfortable, alarmed even, but I pushed that away and hugged my best friend back.

"I missed you," he said into my ear.

"I missed you too."

Kai broke off the hug, turned, and left my room.

He wasn't gone more than two seconds when I heard a rapping on my window.

CHAPTER THIRTEEN

ADAM WAS standing outside my window, hopping up and down like he was trying to keep warm. He wasn't even wearing a jacket. He gestured frantically at me to open the window. He'd already pulled off the screen.

I did, but only an inch or so. "I thought you had practice," I said, pretending not to notice his distress.

"I left early," he replied, his breath misting in the cold. "Said I had a family thing. Can I come in?"

"Eh, I don't know. I really should clean up a little...." I couldn't help the slight smirk that crept onto my face.

With a growl and a muttered curse, Adam grabbed the window and shoved it open the rest of the way before practically diving inside. He slammed the window closed and sighed with relief.

Well, that was no fun. I barely had a chance to make him squirm. "You forgot to put the screen back."

"I can barely feel my fingers!"

"And?"

He had a dismayed look on his face. "But the screen is outside. In the cold. On the ground. I can't reach it without going back outside!"

"If it was on the window where it was *supposed* to be...."

"But...."

"Or if you used a door like a regular person...."

With a groan and a pout, he turned back to the window. I couldn't keep a straight face any longer.

"I'm just kidding," I said with a laugh, "you don't have to go back out there."

"Oh thank God." There was palpable relief in his voice. He really did look pretty cold.

I went to my bed and grabbed the blanket. "I must say I'm disappointed. Time was, you wouldn't have fallen for something like that. Or at least you would have put up a fight."

"I thought we were trying this new thing where we're nice to each other."

I threw the blanket around his shoulders, started rubbing up and down on his arms to warm him up. "Poppycock."

His face twisted in almost disgusted amusement. "Poppycock? Who the fuck even says that?"

"This guy, that's who. Hey, at least I'm not the one who forgot a jacket, like a fool."

"I forgot to grab it from my locker. My backpack too."

"In that much of a hurry to see me, eh?" I joked.

"Yes."

I was a little taken aback. There was no humor or sarcasm or anything in his voice. Only sincerity. My attempts to generate warmth through friction faltered as I floundered for something to say. I couldn't make a joke in response, not when he was being so honest. Not to mention sweet. I suddenly became very aware of how close we were standing to each other, how intensely he was staring at me, unblinking, though still shivering slightly. In that moment, when time seemed suspended, he leaned in and kissed me. It was perfect.

It was also a trap. While I was distracted, with all my defenses down, Adam took the opportunity to shove his hands under my clothes—one up my shirt, the other into the waistband of my pants.

I let loose a completely undignified squeal. "COLD!" It was quite an understatement. His hands made ice seem cozy. Liquid nitrogen could have taken notes from those fingers. I jumped back, desperate to get away, but he managed to keep his hand in my pants—something I would never have complained about in other circumstances, I assure you. With his frigid grip, he pulled me to him and wrapped his arms around me. For not one second did he let his subzero hands leave my skin.

"I must say I'm disappointed," he said, caricaturing the way I'd said those exact words to him minutes ago. "Time was…."

"Oh shut up. I just took pity on you, 'cause you're so cold. Like, more cold than is possible for any human to ever be. Are you actually a ghost?"

He chuckled. "I was out there for, like, a half an hour."

"Oh God. Why would you do that to yourself?"

He shrugged. "I saw that Malachi was here. I, uh, didn't want to interrupt." He blushed slightly, looking away.

"Uh-huh. You didn't want Kai to see you, isn't that right?" He shrugged, still avoiding my eye. "You don't have to be so secretive. I already told Kai about us—"

"You did *what*?" Adam burst out. I was so completely taken aback by his vehemence and the almost crazed look of panic in his eyes that I took an involuntary step back from him.

"Whoa, dude, calm down. Of course I told him. He's my best friend! I'm not about to start keeping secrets from him. But don't worry, I told him not to tell anyone, and he *won't*. If you can't trust him, at least trust *me*. I know how hard this is, and I promise you won't have to do anything until you're ready, but I won't start lying to the people I love."

Adam was standing there, eyes pressed closed, taking deep breaths like he was trying to calm himself down.

"Are you okay?" I asked. He nodded slowly. "Are you mad at me?" He shook his head.

"Just a little freaked out," he said. "Does anyone else know?"

"Only Mel, but she figured it out on her own, like, weeks ago but didn't say anything until the other day."

Adam smiled wryly. "That explains why she was giving me such a hard time when I asked for your number."

"Ha! When she texted me saying she gave it to you, I just knew she had made the experience as awkward as possible."

"She kept practically shouting '*But what do you need to tell him?*' I almost gave up and ran away." We were both laughing, and I knew the tension had finally passed. Belatedly, I remembered that James P. Hogan also knew about me and Adam, or at least that *something* was happening, even if he didn't know any specifics. But I couldn't tell Adam that now. Not only did Adam seem relieved that only Kai and Mel knew, but also, being on the football team with Adam, James was probably the exact kind of person he would want to keep this a secret from.

"What is it?" I asked, noticing that Adam kept glancing at the door to my room.

"Nothing. It's just.... Are your parents home?"

I grinned at him. "Nope. In fact, they're gone all weekend."

Adam grinned back at me. "Is that so? In that case"—he took a step toward me—"I have a few ideas...."

I leapt back, scrambled across my bed to keep away. "Those hands better be warm by now, or so help me...."

His grin took on a decidedly wicked cast. "You'll just have to find out," he said evilly, and dove across the bed at me, arms outstretched.

I yelped and dashed out of my room, with Adam in hot pursuit—or maybe cold pursuit would be more accurate. As far as plans go, deciding to run away from a football player was not one of my best. I made it as far as the living room before I was expertly tackled. Adam wrapped his arms around my chest and took me down, executing a tight spin in midair so he landed on his back with me on top of him, clutched tightly to his chest. Before I had a chance to recover enough from my surprise to move, he had wrapped his legs around mine, pinning me completely. Not that I would have wanted to get away anyway. Lying on top of him like that, I could feel his massive erection through his jeans. He buried his face in my neck, kissing and sucking, and slipped his hand into my pants, grabbing my rapidly hardening cock.

"Um, guys? I'm still here." I turned my head to look toward the kitchen, where I found Kai sitting at the table. "I had to pee, and then there were cookies...." He held up a half-eaten chocolate chip cookie. Adam hadn't moved since we had heard Kai's voice. His face was hidden in the crook of my neck and his body frozen in place, like he was a kid thinking "if I can't see him, he can't see me," or that Kai was one of the dinosaurs in Jurassic Park whose eyes were only able to detect movement for some reason.

"But I will go," Kai continued. "Now. Hi, Adam. Were you hiding in the closet the whole time I was here, or...." That last bit Kai had mumbled to himself as he rushed out the door, slamming it shut in his haste.

As the echoes of the door shutting reverberated through the room, I held my breath, waiting for Adam's reaction, fearing another outburst. Instead, Adam exploded with laughter. Deep, booming, helpless laughs. I joined in—it *was* pretty hysterical. Adam let go of me to reach up and wipe the tears of laughter out of his eyes. I took advantage of my newfound freedom to spin around so I was lying on top of him again, chest to chest. Adam's laughter died down as he stared up at me.

For a moment, that's all we did. Look at each other. Then, slowly, I bent my head and kissed him softly. His mouth parted beneath mine, and my tongue darted in. Adam wrapped his arms back around me, holding me close, and as the kiss deepened and intensified, he flipped us over, so he was lying on top of me.

I found I was enjoying this. Being manhandled, that is. The tackling, the pinning down, and now getting forcibly flipped, being taken control of. It was hot. I wondered if Adam would enjoy it just as much. So I pushed back, and I was on top again. I grabbed his hands by the wrist and slammed them on the carpet on either side of his head, holding him down. I broke off the kiss and grinned triumphantly at him.

"Think you win that easily, huh?"

I hadn't realized it was a competition, but as long as it was.... "If the shoe fits," I taunted.

With a growl, he pushed me off him—rather effortlessly, I'm a little embarrassed to say—grabbed me around the waist, and pulled me to the ground. But I was a little too fast. I slipped from his grasp and rolled, giving him a smack on the ass on the way. I sprang to my feet, ready for him to make the next move.

"Oh, it's so on now," he said, getting to his feet.

"Bring it, jock boy."

He lunged at me, but I darted away, scoring another smack on his ass. Only he was ready for that and caught my arm. He pulled me to him, grabbed me around the waist, and brought us back to the floor, and laughing, we began to wrestle in earnest. He was definitely stronger than me, but I was faster, and lithe. He'd reach for me, I'd slip away and leap on his back with a yell. He'd throw me off and pin me to the floor, so I'd distract him with a kiss until I could worm my way out of his grasp. At one point, as I was trapped beneath him, I had reached up, pulled on his shirt, and tore it. It had been unintentional, a desperate attempt to escape, but I can't complain at the results. His shirt ripped from collar down the center of his chest almost to his navel.

Adam's eyes grew wide in surprise, and mock outrage. "Oh, you did *not* just…" but I cut him off by giggling and tearing his shirt the rest of the way. Long and slow, the sound of tearing fabric filled the room. "That's it," he said. "Now you're in for it." He ripped my shirt completely off in one quick tug. He bent his head and licked my nipple, which made me gasp and sent a shiver down my spine. Taking advantage of my surprise, he grabbed my pants by the pockets and pulled them down, button popping off. Then he took my boxers by the waistband and tore those off too. Now that I was completely naked, he laid himself back on top of me and kissed me. I tugged, ineffectually, at his jeans, trying to get even. The only effect was to make Adam laugh.

"Looks like I won," he said, smugly. "What's my prize?"

I pulled once more on his pants. "Take these off, and I'll show you," I said. Adam stood up, pulled off his pants and what remained of his torn shirt, and stood there, expectantly, already hard from excitement and anticipation. I stood too, grabbed Adam by his shoulders, steered him to the couch, and pushed him down onto it. I knelt on the floor in front of him. I grabbed his cock and stroked it slowly. He watched me, eyes wide and expectant. "Ready?" I asked, and waited for his nod.

He gasped when I took him into my mouth. I swirled my tongue around the head of his cock, massaging his balls as I bobbed up and down along his shaft. "Oh fuck, Dylan," he moaned. He grabbed my hair and began thrusting, deep into my throat. I felt, distantly, glad for my experience with Kai. I remembered how I had gagged the first time

I had deep-throated him, and Adam was *much* larger. But the thought of Kai only flitted through my head and vanished in an instant, replaced completely with the reality of Adam.

Still taking control, Adam pulled me off his dick, lifted my head to his and kissed me hard, tongue probing deeply into my mouth. "Mmm," he moaned, eyes pressed closed. "Weird."

"What's that," I said, breathless.

"I can taste myself." His eyes snapped open, and he grinned at me. "Now suck that dick, fairy boy."

So I did. Adam's moans grew louder and louder. As I went along, they began to be interspersed with more gasps, and cries of "Fuck, Dylan, Yes!" I would have smiled to hear him call my name with such pleasure, but my mouth was a bit busy. I could feel it as Adam approached climax. His hips thrust with barely contained intensity, grunting with every movement. Then he came, waves of hot cum hitting the back of my throat. Slowly, with great relish, I lapped his cock clean as it grew soft in my mouth, spent.

Adam looked down at me through heavy lidded eyes. He had sunk fully into the couch, breathing heavily. "That was fucking the best," he said.

"Yeah?" I sat next to him.

"Oh fuck yes." He kissed me again, his energy returning as he went. He grabbed my cock and started stroking it. After a minute, he broke off the kiss and looked down at his hand, pumping my dick. He licked his lips, and I shuddered slightly in anticipation. I lay back on the couch, propped my head in my hands to watch him.

Slowly, with great deliberation, he lowered his head to my dick. He licked his lips once again, and looked up at me with a strange mix of hunger and hesitation. As our eyes locked, he licked the head of my cock, then paused. He looked thoughtful, like he was examining the taste, deciding whether it was appealing. I was about to speak, tell him he didn't have to suck me if he didn't want to, if he wasn't ready, but before I could open my mouth, he dove on my cock, sucking it all the way to the base.

He gagged, of course, but that didn't abate his enthusiasm in the slightest. He sucked my dick like a man in the desert given an

ICEE. My eyes practically rolled up into the back of my head with pleasure. After all that had happened, the erotic wrestling, sucking Adam for the first time and tasting his cum, it didn't take long for me to reach my bursting point.

"I'm going to cum," I moaned. My cock came out of Adam's mouth with an audible pop, and with two quick strokes of his hand, he had me cumming rivulets of hot, sticky white all over my abdomen and chest. I lay there, panting, spent, but Adam wasn't quite done. Very tentatively, he dipped the tip of his tongue in the cum pooling on my navel. He made a face and looked up at me.

"Don't like it?" I asked with a laugh.

"I dunno, dude. It's weird." He dipped a finger in it, and shoved it in my face. "You try."

I licked his fingers, laughing at the surprised look on his face. "I feel like I just recycled."

CHAPTER FOURTEEN

"...AND THE rest of the weekend continued pretty much like that." It was Monday, my first day back from my suspension, and I was sitting at the lunch table with Kai and Mel.

Mel was overjoyed to hear about Adam and me. I think it tickled her inner romantic—forbidden love, stolen moments, all that nonsense. Kai, on the other hand, seemed the complete opposite of pleased.

"Gross," he said with a scowl the instant I had finished my story.

"I didn't hear you complaining when *you* were the one getting blown all weekend," Mel snarked.

"HEYO!" Mel and I shouted in unison, high-fiving over the table.

Kai stared at Mel flatly. "I really don't appreciate this whole...."

"Yeah, well," Mel interrupted, "I don't appreciate you cutting me out of your life for the better part of two months."

"HEYO!" This time I was alone in shouting. I held my hand out for a high five that never came. Mel arched an eyebrow at me. "Oh. Yeah. Right. That was me too."

Across the lunchroom, I saw Adam arrive, surrounded by a group of other football players. They got in the lunch line, chatting and laughing in a little clump. Adam distanced himself slightly from the group, looked my way, and gave a smile and a discreet little wave. I waved back, which made Adam turn nervously to his friends to see if they noticed. He didn't look back my way.

"You're okay with that?" Kai said. He nodded in the direction of Adam. He must have seen our interaction.

"For now," I replied, "yes. I know how scary coming out can be. I'm not going to pressure him."

"Right," Kai said, skeptically. "Well, it seems to me that if he really cared about you, he wouldn't try so hard to keep everyone from finding out."

"You're one to talk," Mel said.

"What is that supposed to mean?" Kai snapped back at her. Those two had been at each other's throats all day. It made me wonder what was going on with them.

"You tried just as hard to keep everyone from knowing you and Dylan were fooling around."

"That was different."

"Oh yeah? How."

"I wasn't ashamed to be seen with the only openly gay kid in school."

I finally broke in, stopping their bickering. "When you've spent your whole life living in fear of people rejecting you if they found out the truth, then you can tell me what you think Adam should and should not do. Until then, why don't you let me decide what I'm fine with, okay?"

I couldn't help but snap at Kai there, at the end. Truth was, what he had said struck a note of truth in me—a small sliver of doubt I'd been trying my best to ignore. I was angry at Kai for making me realize it. He looked at me apologetically.

Mel expertly changed the subject, but our lunch never quite got back to normal. The shadow of this unresolved argument hung over us for the rest of the period.

OAK LAKE High, after school was out, was split into two major areas. There was the side with the auditorium and the side with the gym. On the one side, the kids who were passionate about the arts hung out. The drama kids rehearsed there, the music kids played in small groups in the practice rooms, the art teacher always stayed late to give kids access to the paint and clay so they could finish their projects. The other side was the haunt of the football players and cheerleaders, the soccer girls and wrestlers. The two sides rarely intermingled. In between was this abandoned rift of empty classrooms, where no one willingly spent any time after the bell had rung. But today, for the first time, I was going to cross this no-man's-land, betray the auditorium side for the gym side. I had my misgivings. Especially because I wasn't supposed to be seen.

I hung out at the threshold of the gym hallway, sat cross-legged with a textbook open on my knees, watching jock after jock leave the locker room from the corner of my eye, waiting for Adam. I was growing impatient. Nearly everyone from the football team had already passed me. A few had looked at me askance, but most hadn't even noticed.

"That's what I was telling Coach," I heard Adam's voice coming from down the hall, not in the direction of the locker rooms but the other way, from the cafeteria. He and James P. Hogan were walking toward me, carrying sodas. They must have made a detour to the vending machines. "But he…." Adam's voice trailed off when he saw me sitting there. I quickly stood up.

"Well," James said after half a second of awkward silence, "I'm going to hit the showers." They were still wearing their football uniforms and all the pads. "Hey Dylan, glad you're back."

Adam stayed silent until James disappeared into the locker room. He moved half a step closer, looking like he wanted to come in for a kiss, but stayed back. Instead, he held out one of the sodas he was carrying toward me.

"Hi," he said lamely.

"You got me a grape soda? That's my favorite. Thanks. How'd you know?"

He smiled shyly at me and shrugged. "It's the only thing I've ever seen you drink."

"Well, now I just feel predictable." Adam gave a soft laugh, reached out and gave my hand a quick, affectionate squeeze, looking around to make sure no one could see us. "I didn't know where we were supposed to meet, so I've been hanging out here. That's cool, right?"

"Yeah. I figured you might, so I hung back after practice. Couldn't quite shake James, though." He looked down at all his football gear. "I should get changed." He started walking toward the locker room, but stopped when he realized I was following. "What are you doing?"

"Coming with." Adam looked at me uncomfortably, like he wanted to protest but couldn't find the words. "What? No one has come in or out of there for like fifteen minutes. It's probably empty. Besides, I'm a man. I can go in the men's locker room if I want." Adam still looked like he wanted to protest. "Unless you're ashamed to be seen with me...."

"Of course not!" *Take that, Kai.* Adam sighed. "Fine. Just don't...." He stopped abruptly, thinking better of whatever he had been about to say. He turned on his heel and walked in.

"Yeah, you better not finish that sentence," I said as I followed him in.

The men's locker room was empty, like I had predicted. I could hear James P. Hogan moving somewhere back there, but he was behind a couple of banks of lockers. But other than that, we were completely alone. That didn't stop Adam from peering around the corners of the lockers to make sure. I huffed a little in frustration, but didn't say anything. Instead, I settled onto one of the benches to watch Adam change. I wasn't going to argue with a free show.

"Are you coming to the game on Friday?" Adam asked, changing hurriedly, without a hint of the sexy-stripping atmosphere I had hoped for.

"Those are still happening? It's supercold out."

"It's the last game of the season. So will you come?"

I smiled. He couldn't quite keep the excitement out of his voice, as hard as he tried to sound nonchalant. "Sure. I'd love to see you play." I reached out and pinched his bare ass before Adam could pull his boxers on.

He leapt a foot into the air, then turned on me. "Don't do that," Adam whispered fiercely. "Not here." He stepped into his pants and pulled them up hurriedly. "Let's go."

Maybe it was what Kai said that afternoon that had gotten to me, or maybe it was simply a desire to make Adam squirm, but seeing him so uncomfortable at having me around the locker room drove me straight to sarcasm.

"Go now? What, with all these hot guys disrobing around me?" Adam rolled his eyes at me, but I could see a hint of a smile. I made an exaggerated show of looking around. "How could I possibly tear myself away from all this delicious eye candy?" Just then, James P. Hogan came into sight around the lockers, towel wrapped around his waist, heading toward the shower. Right before he stepped out of sight, the towel dropped and I was graced with the sight of a small sliver of that perfect ass disappearing around the corner. "Hold that thought," I said, taking an involuntary step forward.

Adam grabbed me and pulled me back. I hadn't realized I had moved until I felt his hand on my arm. "Ha-ha," he said. "Very funny. Can we go?"

"Two minutes. All I need." I hadn't even turned away from where James P. Hogan had disappeared a moment ago. I felt drawn, like I was a piece of iron and James's naked body a particularly powerful electromagnet.

As I pulled away, Adam's grip slid down my arm until he was holding my hand. He pulled me around to face him. "Dylan, quit playing around. Let's go." He grabbed my other hand. "Please?"

I looked down at our hands. Adam had interlaced our fingers, a very intimate gesture, and very public. And to his credit, for once he wasn't looking around to make sure no one could see.

I relented. "You're just greedy. You want to save all the naked James for yourself."

Adam chuckled. "That's exactly what it is."

"Alright, fine. Let's go." I expected Adam to drop my hands then, but he didn't right away. However, before we left the locker room, he did let go, which was probably for the best. Three of Adam's friends were right outside.

Adam's face paled when he almost ran directly into Will Davis, his most homophobic friend. "The fuck you doing with that faggot, Anderson?" Will demanded. Behind him, Alec reddened slightly in embarrassment and avoided my eyes. Dan went so far as to spread his hands and look at me apologetically. Alec and Dan were nice guys at heart, even if they did suffer from keeping the worst company Oak Lake had to offer. Dan and I had even almost been friends back in middle school when his brother was dating my sister. "You playing for the other team, now? I think I speak for everyone when I say we don't want anyone on *that* team on *our* team, know what I'm saying?" He looked back at Alec and Dan with that self-satisfied grin of someone expecting to be backed up by the people behind him.

Adam's mouth was opening and closing, like it knew it should be talking but his brain hadn't gotten around to supplying it with words yet. I was a little irrationally jealous of Will. I hadn't ever gotten Adam to that level of speechlessness. This wouldn't do, not at all.

"Hey, Alec," I said calmly, as though I hadn't just heard that torrent of homophobic vitriol. "You still have that SAT prep book I loaned you? This idiot," I jerked a thumb at Adam, "convinced me to tutor him too."

"Um, I think it's still at my house," Alec said with a little trepidation, doing his best to ignore the incredulous stare from Will. "Where you left it."

"That's okay. I think I have another at home," I said, and Will's eyes almost popped out of his head as he realized he wasn't going to be getting any support from Alec. He turned to Dan expectantly.

But I beat him to it. "Dan, is Bruce going to be home for Christmas? Helen gets in the twentieth. My parents have been talking about inviting your family over, for old times' sake."

Dan grinned impishly at me. "That sounds like fun. I look forward to it." I was bluffing, and he knew it. His brother Bruce and my sister Helen had had kind of a bad breakup. But he also knew Will was an asshat and probably enjoyed the look of betrayal on his face as much as I did.

Finally I turned to Will. "Oh, hey there, Will. I didn't see you standing there. All alone. Were you saying something?" Will sputtered, no doubt overextending his rather small brain for some kind of comeback. Narcissistic douchebags like him could recover from almost anything except being so completely dismissed. Separate them from their crowd of ego-boosting followers, and they withered pretty quickly. "Thought not."

"What just happened?" Adam asked as we walked away.

"Will needed a quick reminder that no one really likes him. Besides, Alec and Dan are not actually jerks, even if they do suffer from a bad case of follow-the-loudest-asshole-in-the-room-itis."

"But what if that had been Kevin, or Ty? Those guys are even worse than Will." Adam was whispering fiercely. I started to realize just how panicked seeing Will had made him.

"Then I would have thought of something else."

"And what if you hadn't?"

I stopped walking, turned to confront Adam. "What are you saying?"

"Nothing. I just…"

"…Never want to be seen with me?" I supplied.

"No! Only, maybe we should be more careful."

"…About being seen with each other. Okay. Cool. Not like I wanted to spend time with you anyway." I started walking again angrily. "You realize that we have always spent a lot of time together? I used to see you between most of my classes. You'd shout at me across the lunchroom at least twice a week. Everyone is used to us interacting. Even fucking Will. Some people even think we're *friends*, despite us landing each other in detention more times than I can count. The only reason anyone would have to even raise an eyebrow at us is 'cause of *you* acting like I'm your shameful fucking secret."

"I'm not ashamed of you," he protested.

"But I'm still a secret?" Adam looked away. "That's what I thought."

We walked in silence from then on. We got outside, into the nearly empty parking lot. Back by where Adam had parked, a few remaining cars blocked us from the view of anyone who might be looking from school, and Adam took that opportunity to grab hold of my hand. It wasn't exactly an apology, out there where no one could see, but I appreciated the gesture.

"Don't think I'm going to let you off that easily," I muttered.

"I have a few ideas on how I can make it up to you."

"Do you now?"

"Mmhmm."

CHAPTER FIFTEEN

"OKAY, SO what's happening now?"

"The game still hasn't started yet, Dylan," Mel said flatly.

"But there's people all over the field," Kai remarked from the other side of Mel.

"They're warming up." She was clearly starting to get exasperated.

"When do *we* get to warm up?" I asked. "I'm really cold just sitting here."

"Yeah," Kai agreed, "When do we get to jump up and cheer?"

"And what do we cheer *for*?"

"Which team is our team?"

"I think we're red. Mel, are we red?"

"What even *is* football?"

Mel buried her face in her hands. "Oh my God, you two are the most hopeless…." Her head snapped up, and she glared at Kai. "Wait, I thought you watch football all the time?"

"Yeah. I wanted to see how much you would put up with."

"They don't kick the football, right?"

Mel laughed. "Nice try, Dylan."

I guess I'll just have to wait and find out for myself, then.

IN CASE you were wondering, feet do not play a major role in football. Seems to me they could have been a little clearer on that front, perhaps considered a different name entirely.

What *did* play a major role in football, however, were piles of men, and no small amount of ass-slapping. In fact, athleticism practically took a backseat to the almost staggering amount of man-on-man action taking place on the field. Up until then I had assumed, naively, that it was either the love of sport or pure masochism that made Adam put up with all the douchebags and homophobia of the football team, or at least the demands of a father desperately trying to relive his glory years. But by the ninth time I saw him under a pile of hot jocks, the truth had become readily apparent.

"Why did no one tell me about this?" I demanded.

"What, football?" Mel said.

"It's a gay man's paradise!"

"What, *football*?"

"It's almost as good as wrestling, but completely without the risk of awkward erections that everyone can see. Tackled by hot guys, ass-smacking on the sidelines…."

"You have some really strange sexual appetites," Kai said wryly.

"An interesting point from a straight guy who likes to get fucked by another dude," Mel said.

"Harsh. But fair."

The game finished pretty quickly after that. We lost, which I needed explained to me. ("Dude, you do see those giant numbers on that board with 'Score' written on it, right?" "…Shut up, Kai."). I said my good-byes to Kai and Mel and hurried over to wait for Adam to get out of the locker room.

I waited outside, at the side exit near the gym, where I knew the team would be leaving on their way to the parking lot. Parents and friends of the players stood around me in loose clumps, chatting quietly, subdued no doubt by the loss. I found a spot out of the way, where I could see when Adam walked out the door, but where I wouldn't draw too much attention.

A shriek split the relatively calm evening. "Oh my *God*!" I turned to see Tiffany jogging over to me, a clump of other cheerleaders not far behind. "I can't believe you came! I've been trying to get you to come see us cheer for*ever*, and you come on the very last game, you bitch!" She was still wearing her tiny cheer outfit as though in defiance of the cold.

I smiled despite myself. Sure, Tiffany was pretty annoying, but her enthusiasm was also rather infectious. "I couldn't miss seeing my bitches cheer, could I?"

"Were we fierce?"

"Superfierce."

"Beyoncé fierce, or like 'last few contestants of *So You Think You Can Dance* when it gets really good' fierce?"

"Um…." I had no idea how to respond to that. There were degrees of fierce? And which one was better? Tiffany, as much as I liked her, happened to be one of those girls where the vaguest implication of an insult, or even merely a lackluster compliment, would send her spiraling into some stygian depths of self-doubt. It would be fascinating if it weren't quite as terrifying to watch. Luckily, the rest of the cheerleaders caught up to Tiffany and rescued me from having to answer.

"Dylan!" Charlotte's face broke into a wide grin. "It's been so long since we've seen you." The other girls echoed her.

"Oh my God," Tiffany turned to Charlotte, face lighting up with even more excitement, as impossible as that seemed. "I have the best idea *ever*. Dylan should come tonight!"

"Oh my God, Tiffany, you are *literally* reading my mind right now!" Amanda, the bustiest, blondest cheerleader exclaimed. "Can he, Char?"

"Sounds like fun to me," Charlotte replied, the only presence of calm in the midst of the tumult of excessively girly excitement. "The girls are all coming over to my house to sleep over tonight. You want to come?"

"Um…." I looked over at the door where half the team had already exited, and any second now Adam would walk out.

"We are not taking 'no' for an answer!" Tiffany said. "It has been *weeks* since we last hung out. I have so much to tell you."

Right then, Adam walked out of the school with a few of his teammates. A group of his friends immediately surrounded him. He chatted with them distractedly, all the while looking over their heads, searching the crowd. He finally noticed me, surrounded by the gaggle of cheerleaders, literally being dragged away by force. His grin split his face nearly in two at the sight of my plight.

Help me, I mouthed at him.

He only winked, smiled wider, and turned back to his friends.

So much for Prince Charming, am I right?

CHARLOTTE'S PARENTS weren't home, which seemed to happen with almost conspicuous frequency. Sure, I'd only been to her house twice before, but every time we all had a free run of the place. Three for three, I'd almost be concerned—if it were anyone other than Charlotte. Even when the group spread to multiple rooms, which, with nearly a dozen teenage girls, happened all too often, she managed to flit effortlessly between rooms, expertly inserting coasters under drinks and somehow catching tipped-over snack bowls before the Chex Mix spilled all over the floor. And that's not even mentioning her juggling of the cooking, music playing, and drama-busting. That last one was especially a marvel to watch. With so many huge personalities in one room, and all of them made up of popular girls who sometimes seemed to subsist entirely on narcissism and cattiness, no sooner would an argument start to think about bubbling than Charlotte would swoop in and work her magic, easing nerves, soothing egos, and just generally reminding everyone that they were friends and were supposed to be having fun.

James P. Hogan should really go into politics, or something that necessitated huge, expensive galas and the like, because Charlotte seemed born to run them.

By ten p.m., the party had pretty much wound down. Most of the cheer squad had dissipated throughout the night, until only five remained, presumably Charlotte's closest friends. And me. At this time, pajamas became the outfit of choice. They even produced a pair for me, an obnoxiously pink-and-kitten-covered pair of matching bottoms and top, which Charlotte insisted was the only type she owned, and she convinced me to wear them in the nicest, politest bout of bullying I have ever had the pleasure to be on the receiving end of. Later that night, when she appeared wearing a perfectly plain pair of flannel pajama bottoms and sweatshirt, she only smiled sweetly (way *too* sweetly) and insisted she had no idea what I was talking about.

We were all sitting in Charlotte's living room, swaddled in blankets. We had finished watching a movie—a romantic comedy of the sappiest variety, of course—and the conversation turned to boys.

"There's someone I've been spending more and more time with lately," Tiffany was saying, smiling coyly. "You'll never guess who."

"Travis Butler," said this girl Mary snidely. Travis was one of the nerdiest guys at school, leader of the physics club, probably the valedictorian of my class, face covered in pimples and painfully awkward around girls. He was also really nice, and happy to help anyone who was struggling in math class, even if that kid had just come out of the closet and most everyone else at the school still acted like he was some weird mix of dinosaur and leper—something they never thought they'd see in the flesh, and quite possibly dangerous.

It made me pretty uncomfortable to hear him be the butt of a joke. I looked around for Charlotte, hoping she'd chime in a delicate reprimand like she had so often already that night, but she was down in the kitchen.

Tiffany's face screwed up in exaggerated disgust. "Ew, no. I'll give you a hint: he's the hottest guy in school." I felt a sinking in my stomach as I started to remember who Tiffany considered to be the hottest guy in school.

"You don't mean…!" Amanda said.

"Yes! Adam Anderson! Every day this week he meets me at my locker and we walk together to practice and he shows me off to all of his friends, 'cause I'm such a catch."

"You?" Mary broke in again, voice dripping with derision. "You have got to be kidding."

Tiffany drew herself up. "What is that supposed to mean?"

Mary raised her eyebrows and gave Tiffany a long look from head to toe. "Girl, don't act like you don't know. Ain't no way someone as hot as Adam would go for all that." She waved a hand at Tiffany.

I took this opportunity to slip out of the room, before I inevitably got pulled into this argument. I felt sick, partly because things had so rapidly dissolved from a friendly conversation to bitchfest of the year, but mostly because of what Tiffany had said about Adam. I felt a lot of conflicting things all at once. I mean, confused snarl of emotions aside, I knew exactly what was going on. The closer Adam and I got, the more terrified he became of people finding out about him, so he was obviously using Tiffany as a cover for his friends, showing them a girl so they wouldn't get suspicious. That didn't stop me from feeling jealous, however. And guilty, like it was my fault he was lying to Tiffany and leading her on.

I had been wandering around the house, not really sure where I was going, but soon found myself approaching the kitchen, where Charlotte was hard at work, baking the cookies we had all so fervently demanded as the movie ended.

"How's it going up there?" Charlotte asked as I sat down at the counter.

"Mary's being a bitch. Again." Charlotte's calm, composed demeanor really encouraged honesty. Normally I wouldn't be quite so brutally honest about someone's friend.

Charlotte wasn't offended. She rolled her eyes and gave an exasperated sigh. "She's had a stick up her ass for the last two weeks, and I can't figure out why. She being a bitch to Tiffany again?" I nodded. "Typical. Well, I hope you're having fun at least."

"Oh yeah. I am."

Charlotte popped a ball of cookie dough into her mouth and turned to me, eyebrow raised. "But?"

Damn she was perceptive. Nobody other than Kai and Mel had ever really been able to tell when I was holding something back. "I don't know. It's just… like, I feel this demand to be someone I'm not. Or at least, not usually. I mean, it's fun sometimes to be the sassy gay guy in the popular clique, or whatever, but it's exhausting."

Charlotte handed me a spoonful of the cookie dough, which I gladly accepted. "The thing about these girls is they've been raised on *Sex and the City* and the like. They've grown up dreaming of a Gay Best Friend to call their own and, well, I'm sorry to say it, but you are the one who decided to come out and become the object of their obsession," she said with a smirk and a wink.

I laughed. "How foolish of me, coming out like that."

"A shameful grab for popularity if ever I saw one," she joked. The oven beeped, and Charlotte pulled out a sheet of freshly done cookies. Practically before I could even smell their delicious, chocolate-chippy goodness, she had poured two glasses of milk and deposited a small plate of cookies on the counter between us.

Damn she was good.

"They're best right out of the oven. You just have to be fast and take a drink of milk so you don't burn your tongue." She demonstrated, popping an entire cookie into her mouth and downing nearly the entire glass of milk. Then she grinned at me, smudges of chocolate staining her teeth. "Best we don't tell those bitches upstairs about that little number, am I right?"

I was a little more conservative about my own cookie. I only shoved my face with half a cookie at a time. "How are you so amazing?"

"It's my mom's recipe and Dad's favorite way of eating them," Charlotte said, tossing another batch into the oven. "I really can't take credit."

"Not that. Though, yes, these cookies are amazing. I mean *you*. You're so chill about me being gay…."

"I have a gay uncle and a lesbian aunt, on opposite sides of my family. I just have a little more practice than everyone else is all."

"Okay, but it's more than that. You're probably the most beautiful girl in school…"

"You flatterer, you."

"…You're definitely the most popular. Head cheerleader, dating the hottest, most popular guy in school…"

"Hottest? You've obviously never seen him in the mornings."

"…But despite that, you're not a shallow bitch like most of the other girls. Not even in an endearing, good-hearted way, like Tiffany is."

Charlotte tilted her head, studying me. She didn't say anything for so long, I started to fear I had gone too far, misjudged how close we were, overestimated how honest I could be.

Finally, she said, "I used to be."

Her expression didn't change. Tentatively, I said, "What changed?"

"My best friend growing up was a girl named Sandy. We were awkward little seminerds together. We grew up, and I started to get pretty, and popular. She stayed awkward. There was this girl Laura—you probably don't remember her; she graduated while you were still in middle school—she was the most popular girl in school, and when I was a freshman, I tried to be exactly like her. She was why I started cheering. I made the team, started following Laura around everywhere, doing my best to imitate her every move. I was not a nice person then." She smiled wryly. "Even James didn't like me. That winter, a little before Christmas, Sandy killed herself. Her suicide note was addressed mostly to me. Sometimes I'm surprised her parents let me read it. It had a lot to say."

I was aghast. Suddenly the distant look in Charlotte's eyes made sense. What surprised me most was how calm she was as she told me. How matter-of-fact. The sadness was there, but it was a distant thing, hidden under acceptance.

"I'm so sorry. I didn't mean to…."

She waved away my apology. "Sometimes I'm glad for it, as terrible as that sounds. It made me take a hard look at myself, who I was becoming. Made me ask myself who I *wanted* to become. I only wish that could have happened before…." For a split second, I thought the sadness would rise up and overtake her, but then the oven beeped and she turned to pull the cookies out.

"Besides," she continued, the lightness I had come to associate with her returning to her voice, "it turns out people respond more to niceness than to cruelty, and I'm much better at it. So I stayed popular. Maybe even became more so. I'm sure it helped that I'm 'probably the most beautiful girl in school,' as you put it. The other girls, who craved popularity as fervently as I used to, tried to take me down, assert their superiority with mean words and actions. That's how girls typically get popular, you see, by making other girls feel like shit so they retreat, follow the mean girl's lead, and stop competing in this terrible game we call high school. But they couldn't hurt me, so they never won. Far worse had been said by someone I cared about way more. Someone I'd lost the chance to reconcile with." She once again stuffed an entire cookie into her mouth and drained the rest of her glass of milk. "Sandy used to love eating cookies like that." She grinned, no doubt remembering those happy times.

"Thanks for sharing that with me."

"Of course. We're friends, aren't we?"

We really were. Like, real friends. I felt myself compelled to tell her about Adam, share with her my misgivings. All the doubt I'd been having lately, feeling like his shameful secret. It seemed like she might have something insightful to say, some way I could make the situation easier. But at the same time, I knew I couldn't tell her about it, not without betraying Adam, at least a little bit. Which is exactly what I was upset about, this need to keep quiet. It was frustrating.

So I ate another cookie, and thought of something benign to say. "Tonight's been fun. You really know how to throw a party."

"You should come to my New Year's party. Everyone's invited, and most of the school comes. It's awesome."

As we gathered up the cookies and headed back to the group, a plan was forming. Charlotte's New Year's party was the perfect solution to my problem. Everyone would be there, so no one would think twice about Adam and me both being there. We could spend time together in front of everyone. We'd show everyone we were friends, so we wouldn't have to be quite as secretive. Maybe we could even sneak off to some secluded corner, where no one was around to see us, and enjoy some of our more… private activities.

And if someone did catch us, and the secret was out? Well, I couldn't say I'd be too upset.

CHAPTER SIXTEEN

"...WELL, ANYWAY, I was thinking, since Charlotte's New Year's parties are always so huge—like the entire junior and senior classes will probably be there—it wouldn't be weird at all for us both to be there. And since practically everyone knows we've been hanging out lately anyway—okay, okay, that I've been 'tutoring' you, but still. What I'm saying is, I think we should go together. It would be fun."

Adam took a long time to finish chewing his bite of sandwich. We were at Adam's secret spot, what I still referred to as Adam's Lake, even though he had told me its real name at least three times. It had taken me a few weeks to work up the courage to finally broach the subject with him. A few weeks of practicing speeches in mirrors, and case-testing them with Mel, all thrown out the window the instant I opened my mouth and began stammering. Typical.

Adam finally swallowed. "I can't. I have family stuff to do that night. We're visiting my mom. Besides, I figured you'd wanna spend that time with your friends. Hasn't Kai been complaining lately that you two never hang out?"

Kai really had. He'd started periodically sending me texts listing things that had happened more recently than us hanging out. The last one was *Dinosaurs went extinct*. "Yeah, I guess."

"There you go. I can spend time with my family. You can hang out with your friends. Everyone's happy. And then after that, maybe you and I can have our own private celebration here."

"In January? Maybe we could find someplace else. Someplace a little more *indoors*."

"Oh come on. It won't be so bad. We could build an igloo, hunker down for the winter."

"Or, we could do it at my house, where there's heat."

"But there's so much more we can do out here, where it's private."

Great. Private. Always private. "Oh yeah? Like what?"

"I can think of a few things." He grinned at me suggestively. "In fact, why wait until January? We could get started right now."

"Now? It's like thirty-five degrees out here. And we can't exactly build that igloo, unless you're hiding a bunch of snow in your pants."

"There's always the back of my car."

My eyes narrowed. "You're trying to change the subject, aren't you?"

"Is it working?"

"Oh yeah. Now go get the car started so it can warm up."

"No need. We can get it steamy enough on our own."

BEFORE CLASS started, I broached the subject of New Year's with Kai.

"I thought you already had plans" was his immediate, biting response.

I knew he wasn't gonna make this easy. "I simply thought it's been so long since we've hung out. Why don't I spend the holidays with my best friends? Besides, wasn't hanging out on New Year's your idea?"

"Yeah, and I believe your exact words when I had the idea were 'ha-ha, no. I'm going to Charlotte's party.'"

"You're taking my words out of context," I said.

"'Everyone who is *anyone* is going to be there, which you'd know if you'd gotten invited,'" he continued.

"Okay, I'm pretty sure you're paraphrasing."

"'This my chance, blah blah, popular kids, blah blah, finally be cool, new best friends, etc., etc.'"

That last part wasn't even *close*. "Is that really how I sound to you?"

"Pretty much."

"And are we suddenly in a teen movie? Are we the misfit kids desperate for popularity with, like, a 'lose our virginity by prom' pact? 'Cause I can think of like twelve reasons why that doesn't work off the top of my head."

Kai shrugged. "It's the only reason I can think of why you're so desperate to go to this party."

"You're right. I was popularity crazed. But now I've come to my senses, and we can hang out, just us misfits."

"Unless…." Kai's eyes narrowed. "You wanted to go with Adam, but he doesn't want to go with you."

Fuck. I was really beginning to wish I had stupider friends. "Well, yes and no."

"What does that mean?"

"Yes, he doesn't want to go, and, um, no, I'd rather just spend the night with you?"

"Let me get this straight." Kai said. "Because Adam's not going, now suddenly you don't want to either?"

"I mean, when you put it that way, it sounds kind of…."

"No, that makes perfect sense." His words practically dripped with sarcasm.

"Really? 'Cause your words are saying one thing, but your tone is saying another."

"I mean, why would you want to go? You don't have anyone to go with."

"I feel like we've established that already."

"You don't know a single other person you could take. Nope, not a one."

"Okay. I think I see where this is going."

"It's not like there's anyone you've been friends with since forever…"

"Kai…."

"…Who has always wanted to go to a cheerleader party…"

"First I'm hearing about it."

"…'Cause he's been trying to make it with Sandra for, like, ever…."

"I remember things a little bit differently. One might say gayer."

"Someone who has stuck by your side through thick and thin, good times and bad…."

I sighed. "Kai, do you want to go to Charlotte's party?"

"What, me? I'd have to check my schedule," Kai said with a mixed look of smugness and feigned innocence, and a grin like he thought he was clever. It was embarrassingly satisfying when, a second later, Mel dropped her books on the desk behind him, making him jump slightly in surprise. Try and play that one cool, doofus.

"The weirdest thing just happened to me," Mel said as she sat down.

"What's that?" Kai asked, turning his startled jump into a pretend stretch. No one was fooled.

"Out in the hall, I was banked by a horde of cheerleaders. Before I knew what was happening, I was right outside the lunchroom where Charlotte Pierce herself made a big deal about asking me to come to her New Year's Eve party. She was, like, really weirdly insistent. She mentioned your name, Dylan, no less than six times. I counted. I found myself saying yes, simply because she was so oppressively nice to me. I'm not certain I was physically capable of saying no. I made it halfway back here before I noticed I was carrying a bag of homemade cookies and a personalized thank-you note."

"Do you still have those cookies?" Kai asked, "'Cause I know a guy who…." Mel handed him a cookie, and he shoved the whole thing in his mouth. "Ooo, they're good."

"Dylan, I think she might legit be an evil genius," Mel said.

"Maybe she just really wants you to come," I said.

"No. I go to Charlotte's New Year's party every year. That's not what this is."

"Seriously?" Kai said. "Am I the only one who doesn't get invited to this thing?"

Mel ignored him. "I get the feeling she went to this length so I would convince you to come, Dylan."

"What about me?" Kai whined. "I want to come."

"No, Malachi. She specifically said you're not invited." Mel said dryly. "The only thing I can't figure out," she continued, ignoring Kai's sulk, "is why she would be worried you wouldn't come. The other night you were really excited to go."

"Oh, you know," I said, "I thought it might be more fun if we did something just the three of us. How long has it been since the gang's been together, am I right?"

Mel gave me a flat look. "Let me guess," she said to Kai, "Adam doesn't want to go, so now Dylan wants to stay home and mope."

"What is with the both of you and…?" I began, indignant.

"That's exactly what it is," Kai said, cutting me off.

"I figured. Listen, Dylan, I know it bothers you that Adam doesn't want to be seen with you in public…."

"What? That is *not* why I don't want to go to Charlotte's party." Both Mel and Kai gave me identical "really?" looks, down to the angle of their raised eyebrows. They *had* to have practiced that. "Okay, maybe that's a tiny part of it."

"Exactly," Mel continued. "And you knew that was the deal going into this. You've even said that you were okay with that, how many times?"

"I don't know…."

"At least a million," said Kai.

"Oh come on, it wasn't that many."

"At. Least. A. Million," Mel reiterated. "So you are in no way allowed to mope about this. You are coming to this party with me."

I sighed. Clearly I'd lost the argument. No sense in putting up a fight. It was a very real possibility that Mel would literally drag me to this party. She'd done it before.

"Well, I guess it *would* be fun to party with you."

"Damn straight it will be."

"Just to be clear," Kai said, "I am coming to this party too, right?"

"We'll see," I said.

"If you're good," Mel said.

We laughed.

"No, but seriously, I get to come, right? Guys? Stop laughing at me! I'm starting to feel insecure. Seriously? That makes you laugh harder? … I hate you guys."

CHAPTER SEVENTEEN

WHEN NEW Year's Eve finally rolled around, I wasn't sure what to expect. I had never been to one of those high school megaparties before. Sure, Oak Lake was a small school, but if it was true that most of the junior and senior classes were coming, even if they did filter in and out throughout the night, that still meant there'd be hundreds of kids there.

Now, Charlotte's house was easily big enough to swallow crowds of people, but I imagined it had to be overflowing. I mean, I really just had movies and TV shows to go off here. I was picturing walls shaking as enormous speakers pumped out dance music, discarded beer cans, and drunken teens rollicking around the yard, broken windows with scantily clad people hanging out of them. That whole schtick.

Imagine my surprise when I showed up with Mel and Kai, and the only signs of a party were the lights in every window, and the occasional silhouette. Well, that and all the cars parked on the street. We had to circle around for about twenty minutes before we found a place to park over a block away.

"Not what I was expecting," Kai said. I grunted in agreement.

"You were thinking it would be a rager?" Mel asked.

"Well, yeah. Basically."

Mel shook her head. "Charlotte always throws classy affairs."

"Seriously, how did I never know about you going to these parties?" Kai asked.

"There's a lot of things you don't know about me. I'm a big ball of mystery."

"Right," Kai said dryly. "Obviously. So what do we do, knock or just burst in and join the mass of lithe and youthful bodies?"

"What do you mean, we?" I joked as we walked up to the door. "You were just our ride. You can leave now."

"Ha, ha. Very funny," Kai said sarcastically as Mel knocked.

Charlotte opened the door. "Welcome to my New Year's extravaganza! Where the fun...." She cut off when she saw who was at the door. "Malachi," she said in a tone the dripped with scorn. She turned to Mel and me. "I thought I made it clear that *he* was in no way allowed to step foot in my house *ever*. He is the vilest, least popular scum to ever crawl the halls of Oak Lake." With each word, Kai's jaw dropped lower and his face grew redder until he looked like an anthropomorphic tomato about to eat a bowling ball.

Mel and I burst out laughing in unison, and Charlotte's face went from wrathful to grinning in a fraction of a second. Kai's mouth snapped close with an audible click.

"What just happened?" he asked.

"They told me to give you a hard time, hon," Charlotte replied. "Apparently you are the only person in the entire school who didn't know my parties are open invitation. Couldn't pass that opportunity up, and man, was it worth it." She held out her hand. "Now, keys please."

Kai, who was busy glaring at Mel and me, was taken completely off guard by Charlotte's demand. "What?"

"Your car keys. Give them to me. I do my best, but my punch always ends up spiked and the jocks manage to smuggle in beer. I suspect in their pants, but I'm not about to mandate strip searches upon entry—as much as we'd all enjoy it, I'm sure. Point is, when you're ready to leave, you can get your keys back from me once sobriety has been proven." She wiggled her fingers expectantly. Kai heaved an exaggerated sigh, but dropped his keys in her hand. "Now, welcome to the party!"

Inside, things were much more like what I was expecting. The living room was absolutely packed with people. Nearly everyone held a red Solo cup. Music played and people danced and filtered from room to room to experience everything the party had to offer. The kitchen was stuffed with mostly jocks, engaging in drinking competitions to the sound of "Chug! Chug!" shouted at the top of their lungs. An office was packed with nearly two-dozen people watching fail videos on YouTube and laughing uproariously. A group chilled at the end of a hall, smoking near an open window.

In short, the party was *awesome*. Whenever things would start to get out of hand—say the music got so loud eardrums could burst or a fight began to brew—Charlotte would materialize and flawlessly deal with the issue, redirecting everyone to the fun and celebration. She'd snatch drinks in midair before they could spill, replace ashtrays, and subtly make certain all the smoke made it *out* the window, all with a smile and enough charm to melt the iciest heart. And don't even get me started on her ability to dispense snacks. You'd have an empty hand for a fraction of a second, and BAM there'd be a plate full of all your favorite foods. She was magic.

Right when we got inside, Kai immediately dove into the tangled limbs and bodies on the dance floor, grinding up on every girl who would tolerate his attentions. It would have been creepy if it weren't for his endearing enthusiasm, which was apparently enough for most of the girls to not only tolerate, but welcome his eager undulations.

For a moment—just a moment, like a split second, I swear—I actually felt a little jealous. Not because I wanted to be the one Kai was grinding up on (okay, that was a little bit of it, teensy, honest), but because he had someone to dance with. Sure, I could have danced with Mel, or one of my cheerleader friends, but not that crotch-bumping, sexual-energy-fueled kind of dancing Kai was indulging in with such reckless abandon, with no less than *three* girls simultaneously, for the record. Even if I had been able to convince Adam to come with me, that would still have been off limits. In fact, having him there might have made this even *more* frustrating. Realizing that left a sour taste in my mouth and a kink in my gut. But I was determined not to let it get to me. So Mel and I ran off to experience the rest of the party, with all the brimming enthusiasm of two coked-out kids at a carnival.

Upstairs the party had taken on an entirely different tone. The music could still be heard from downstairs, but muted, as were all the sounds of the party. Small groups gathered together for close-knit conversations on everything from school gossip to who would win in a fight between Batman and Spiderman. I weighed in on that last one, in favor of Spiderman, obviously, provided we discounted the various bat-vehicles. It grew quite heated there for a while. Mel had to drag me away before I punched someone in his stupid, bat-loving face.

I walked into one room that was pitch black. Luckily my ears registered the, shall we say, intimate sounds before my hand managed to find the light switch. By the light from the hallway, I could see a small bowl filled with condoms sitting on a table. I recognized Charlotte's trademark touch—uncannily prepared for every eventuality. Though, if my ears were as good at determining the sheer number of people in that room as I believe there were, then Charlotte better have another one of those bowls stashed somewhere, or there was a real danger of running out. I pulled the door shut, but paused for a moment before I took my hand off the doorknob. As dark as it was in there, I could easily sneak in and join the fun without any guy realizing that I wasn't exactly a girl. I noticed Mel giving me a knowing look. I quickly let go and walked away.

I mean, I wouldn't have actually done it. Sure, I was feeling a little miffed about Adam not being there, and just generally about being the gay dude outside the straight people's all-you-can-eat buffet, but I wasn't about to go hurting the guy who was becoming more and more important to me by the day. I only wanted to, you know, let that possibility sink in so I could bring it back up when I was alone, in the shower perhaps. Or reenact the fantasy later with Adam.

Of course, it would have been even better if Adam had been there, and we could have actually *done* it. Right there, in front of everyone, without anyone knowing. But this was not the time to dwell on that. This was a *party*, dammit, and Mel and I were going to rock it.

We danced with Kai until our ears wanted to bleed from the music, which, despite Charlotte's best efforts, kept climbing higher. We won a doubles Ping-Pong tournament against two kids from the physics club. Mel even beat Will Davis at a beer-chugging contest, and the rest of the football team lifted her on their shoulders and carried her around. At one point I joked to Mel that this night was so extreme there would even be a party going on in the front closet. I threw open the door and interrupted two people in the middle of a very personal sort of party. I couldn't tell who one of them was—he jumped behind the hanging coats too fast for me to make out anything more than black hair and that he was very definitely a guy. The other one I recognized immediately.

"It's you," I said. "That kid I rescued from Adam way back at the beginning of the year. I guess he was right about you. How does he always fucking do that? What are you even doing here? Freshmen aren't supposed to be at this party, much less in the closet…." I noticed the terrified, caught look on his face, and changed what I was about to say. "Completely alone. With your pants unbuttoned. All by yourself." The kid's look vacillated between surprise, confusion, and relief almost too fast to follow. "Excuse me," I said, and closed the door, shutting the two secret lovers back in.

That was it. The last straw. The final bit of missed gay opportunity that I could deal with for one night. It was supposed to be me and Adam secretly making out in a closet, goddammit, not some fucking faceless whoever and that goddamned new-kid freshman.

We were supposed to feel the adrenaline haze of risky loving, with fear of getting caught only fueling our need. *I* was the one who fucking came out and dealt with all these bullshit people for years, not once getting so much as a lustful glance along the way, and this stupid freshman comes along out of the blue and immediately gets play? Meanwhile I have to be the one alone at the party, again, surrounded by straight people having the time of their fucking lives.

"Are you okay?" Mel asked, clearly having noticed the rage that boiled within me. I know she meant well, but it only made me madder. Suddenly I saw the entire night in a whole new light. While that stupid fucking freshman was running around with his forbidden love, probably sneaking touches on the dance floor and exchanging longing glances over the Ping-Pong table before dashing off to give in to temptation in the closet, I was spending my night with a fucking *woman*. Sure, she was my best friend and I loved her, like, a lot, but I was so tired of my right-hand man not being, well, a *man*. I felt sick. It was hard to see the night I'd spent with Mel as fun anymore. All I could think of was how that freshman stole the night I should have had with Adam.

"I'm fine. I'm just done with this party. Can we leave?"

Mel's brow furrowed with concern. She clearly didn't believe I was fine, but knew that I wasn't going to be talking about it here. "Sure," she said. "Let's find Kai."

That was easy. Kai was right where we'd left him, making a fool of himself on the dance floor.

"Already?" he asked when I said I wanted to leave. "But we just got here!"

"It's been like four hours," I said.

"But…." He looked from me to the girls on the dance floor and back. He gave a look like a begging puppy. Before I could say anything, Mel grabbed his arm and whispered something in his ear. He rolled his eyes. "Fine," he said. "Let's go." We were heading to the front door when I saw *him*, standing in the corner behind a ficus, talking to Tiffany with that sort of forehead-to-forehead type of conversation that only comes with deep flirting.

It was Adam.

CHAPTER EIGHTEEN

ADAM SAW me too. There was no mistaking it. Our eyes met, and I could see the panic in them. He hid it well, though. I doubt anyone else noticed. Tiffany certainly didn't. She kept talking as before, oblivious to the sudden tension in the air.

Mel saw him too, and gasped. "That bastard," she said.

Kai was a little slower on the uptake. "I though you said he couldn't make it? Wait, why is he with…?" His brain must have finally caught up to his mouth. "Oh. *Oh.* That bastard."

"Do you want Kai to punch him?" Mel asked.

"Yeah, do you want me to…. Wait, why do *I* have to be the one to punch him? Dude's huge!"

"Ladies never punch."

"You punch *me* all the time."

"It's okay, guys," I said. "I got this."

I made straight for them, but I ignored Adam. Instead I focused on Tiffany. "Oh my *God*, bitch. Where have you been all night? You look fierce. Spin for me, babe. Let me see that little black number." She did so, beaming at the attention. "Girl, what are you looking all pretty for?"

"Oh, you know," she said, wrapping her arms around Adam's bicep. "Always gotta look my best." She looked up at Adam coyly. "Never know when it will come in handy." She put a special emphasis on the word "handy" like she was going for some kind of innuendo. Adam gave no sign he noticed her attentions. His eyes were glued on me.

I didn't so much as bat a single eyelash his way. "Work it, girl. I'm going to dance. Adam." I gave him the slightest of nods, acknowledging his presence, barely, for the first time. Then I turned and walked back to Mel and Kai. I could feel Adam's eyes on me the whole way.

A rational human would be forgiven for expecting something a little more confrontational from me. And I'm not saying I didn't have that desire. I'd be lying if I said there wasn't a small part of me that wanted nothing more than to confront him, loudly, in front of everyone. But that was only a small part of me. The thing is, even pissed as I was, I cared about Adam. I didn't want to hurt him. Well, no, that's not true, I did want to hurt him. But, like, a small hurt. A punch-in-the-gut, maybe even the knock-the-breath-from-him kind of hurt. Not the colossal, world-stopping, soul-rending kind of pain that would happen if I outed him right then. I didn't want him to feel that fear. A hint of that fear, sure, as he worried whether I would out him or not—but I wouldn't actually do it.

Besides, if I did, he would have something to be mad at me for. Something legitimate he could blame on me. And I wanted him to wallow in the totality of his guilt.

So I simply walked back to Mel, who was looking at me with admiration in her eyes, and Kai, who was looking at me in shock.

"What just happened?" Kai asked.

"That was diabolical," Mel said.

"Who even *are* you?" Kai was dumbfounded.

I ignored him. Instead, I said to Mel, "Do you think you could…?"

"Already on it," she said. She reached out and grabbed Miranda Brickmann's arm, who was walking by right at that moment. "Oh my God, Miranda!" she said, joining her in walking toward the kitchen. "I'm so glad you came! Good. I say fuck him."

"What do you mean?" Miranda asked.

"You didn't know? Oh God, I'm so sorry. Forget I said anything." If I didn't know Mel even half as well as I did, it would be remarkable how sincere she sounded in all this.

"No, tell me. What is it?" Just like that, Miranda had gone from slightly confused to full-on concerned.

"It's nothing. It's just, I heard that Adam was going to ask you to this party, but apparently…." Her voice faded into the general din of the party as they walked away.

Kai was still staring at me, wide-eyed, like he had never seen me before. "What? Playing the sassy gay best friend is fun, sometimes," I said, guessing what had thrown him for such a loop.

"Okay," he said. "Sure. But what's this that's happening, right now?"

"Oh. That. Well, I gave Tiffany the encouragement she needed to throw herself completely at Adam. Figure if he wants to pretend to be straight, he can damn well deal with the ramifications of that. Presumably Mel is doing the same thing with Miranda, and probably Caroline. And almost definitely Samantha."

"Did you two plan this?"

"No, we just make a really good team, especially when it comes to spinning elaborate lies in tandem."

"Well, a lot of things suddenly make sense in hindsight," Kai mumbled to himself. "Okay, but am I the only one who worries that this is, well, kind of evil?"

Before I could formulate an answer, James P. Hogan appeared around the corner. "Dylan! Malachi! How's the party?" he exclaimed, putting a hand on each of our shoulders and squeezing.

It was a sign of my mental state that James's close proximity and affectionate physical contact didn't trigger an immediate bout of giddiness. I barely even noticed the heady scent of cologne tinged with sweat, or the tantalizing way his muscles rippled in his forearm.

Barely.

"It's a great party," I replied.

"Swell," Kai said, without taking his narrowed eyes off me.

"Okay...," James said suspiciously. "I'm missing something here." Right then, he noticed Adam, still in the same corner with a heavily flirtatious Tiffany. Only now Miranda was there too, latched to his other arm. It was a neck-to-neck flirtation war. A few other girls were starting to gather around the edges, some even throwing themselves into the fray.

"Oh my God," James said, letting go of Kai, grabbing my shoulders and turning me toward him—and away from Adam. "Are you okay? Did you two split? What happened?" He was looking at me with genuine concern.

I swooned a little. I'm only human. "I'm okay. It's under control."

"Wait, *he* knows?" Kai broke in, incredulous. "He didn't know before me, did he?"

"Well," I said, "I mean… he figured it out…."

"I can't believe—" Kai started.

"What do you mean, under control?" James began.

Mel showed up, interrupting them both. "Operation Raining Bitches is a go," she said with a self-satisfied smirk.

I turned and found Adam drowning in a sea of girls, each desperate to get their hands on him. "Holy shit! How did you do it?"

"Trade secrets," she said.

"Remind me never to piss you off," Kai said.

"That was something you were in danger of forgetting?" Mel replied sweetly. Too sweetly.

"You guys did this?" James asked. "Uh-oh. Charlotte is *not* going to be happy."

As though invoking her name summoned her, Charlotte materialized at James's elbow. "Hon," she said, a dangerous edge to her voice. "Why do I sense drama at my party? I've worked *very* hard to keep all the drama *out* of this party." Her eyes took in the expressions on all our faces, then quickly glanced once over at Adam. Finally, her gaze settled on me and, in those eyes, I saw my doom. "I see. Revenge drama, is it?"

"Wait," I said. "You know?"

"She does?" Mel and Kai said in unison with identical amounts of surprise and jealousy.

"You told her?" I said accusingly to James.

"Actually, I told him," Charlotte said.

James shrugged at me with a look that said "What? We both know I'm not the smart one in this relationship."

"That's not the point," Charlotte continued. "Melanie, you promised me you wouldn't use your powers for evil."

"What makes you think it was me?" Mel said indignantly.

Charlotte turned those doom eyes to her. "I recognize the touch." Mel visibly withered.

"I'm sensing a story here I wish I knew," Kai whispered to me.

"I know," Mel said, sounding halfway to apologetic, "I remember what happened last time—"

"*Really* wish I knew."

"—but when you mess with the people I love, the claws come out. Sorry I'm not sorry."

Charlotte turned back to me. "Dylan, I expected better from you. I'm going to have to ask you to leave."

"That's fine," I said before anyone could protest. "We were just leaving, anyway."

CHAPTER NINETEEN

WE GOT back to my house in time to watch the ball drop with my parents. They didn't say anything about our early return, though they exchanged many looks. Probably had something to do with Mel and Kai's uncharacteristic silence. Or maybe the grim look on my face. Afterward, the three of us headed to my room to play video games. After a few halfhearted rounds of losing, I quit and let Mel and Kai play on their own. The way I figured it, there was no need to ruin their fun with my sour mood.

Before we had been home much longer than an hour or two, there was a noise at my window. In unison, Mel and Kai looked at each other, then at me, then dove behind my bed, out of sight. The knocking came again.

I threw back the curtain and opened the window, only a few inches. "What?"

"Let me in." It was Adam—as if there could have been any doubt.

"No."

"Come on, Dylan, I just want to talk to you."

"You could always try the front door. But then, that wouldn't be *secret*, would it?"

"Is that what this is about? If you would let me explain—"

"That's not what this is about."

Adam growled with frustration and tried to pull off the window screen like he had so many times before. Only this time it didn't budge. "What the…? Did you nail this thing down?"

"Screws, actually. But yes."

"Goddammit…. Dylan, listen, you have every right to be mad, but—"

"Mad? Who's mad? I'm not mad." Lies. But he didn't need to know that.

"Then why the fuck are you doing this? If you'd just let me finish a fucking sentence, maybe I could explain—"

"Explain what?" Okay, I'll be honest, continually cutting him off was giving me *far* too much pleasure right then. Whatever, I felt no shame. "You don't need to explain anything. I understand. Really, I do. You're scared of people finding out you're gay, right?" Adam was staring at me, obviously dumbstruck that I wasn't yelling at him, that I wasn't rising to meet his anger. Instead, I spoke calmly. "Let me guess. You thought people were starting to suspect. Someone—probably Will Davis, am I right?—started giving you shit about how much time you spend with me, how disinterested you seem in girls these days, blah blah blah. So you decided to stop the rumors before they could spread by being seen, very publicly, flirting heavily with a girl. And voila, problem solved. Well? Am I right?"

Adam refused to meet my eyes.

"That's what I thought," I continued. "You know how I knew all that? Because it is *such a fucking cliché*! So I'm not mad at you. I'm not mad that you're scared. I get that. I'm not mad that you want to keep our relationship a secret. I told you I was okay with that. I'm not even mad that you'd go to extravagant lengths to try and prove to everyone you really are straight. I sort of figured going into this there'd be a few of those attempts. But you know what I'm not okay with? Being your kept boy, essentially your mistress. I'm fine with you not telling people about us, but not with being your little affair on the side. And, fuck, Adam, Tiffany is my *friend*, and she really likes you. She doesn't deserve to be your beard. Did you even think about how she would feel when she eventually realizes you don't care for her at all?" I'm a little ashamed to admit that it was only then, saying that to Adam, I realized that I, too, had used Tiffany. In that way, I was no better than Adam. Worse, even, since he was only afraid to tell the truth, but I was acting out of a petty desire for revenge. I'd have to bake a cake or something in apology. But I wasn't about to mention any of that to Adam.

"But do you know what the worst part is, Adam? The part I'm most hard-pressed to overlook? You *lied* to me. If you had told me what you were feeling, I could have helped you through it. At the very least, I could have told you that I'm *not* okay with you pretending to date someone else, that it would end our relationship—"

"Oh, you are really one to talk, Dylan," Adam burst in, rallying his anger and making one more attempt to turn the tables back on me. "Did you tell me before you went and fucked Malachi?"

"There are a million and one reasons why that is different, and you know that full well. For one, I broke it off when I realized how it affected you. Are you prepared to do the same?"

"What—" The anger finally drained from Adam. "What do you want from me?"

"I want you to come through that front door and commit to actually *being* my boyfriend. Or I want you to leave."

For a long while he stood there, staring at me. I could see him teetering on the edge of a decision, but for the life of me, I couldn't figure out where he was going to land. When finally he turned his back and walked away, I knew he'd made his decision. And I knew he didn't choose me.

"What's happening?" came Kai's voice from behind the bed. "Did he say yes? Is he coming in?"

"Oh, you lovable idiot," Mel said. "No." She always was that much quicker on the uptake. The two of them came over and wrapped their arms around me in a group hug. I think they were expecting me to cry. To be honest, I was kind of expecting me to cry, too, at least a little. But all I did was stare out the window at those footprints, barely visible in the snow, feeling hollow.

There was a soft knock at the door. Mel and Kai jumped, no doubt thinking it might be Adam, changed his mind or come to his senses or something. I knew better. Regardless, it was still a slight surprise when my mom poked her head through the door.

"Hey," she said, "I brought you some ice cream. I figured you might need it." She held out a newly opened pint of ice cream with three spoons stuck in it.

I laughed. I couldn't help it. This was just too surreal. It was helpless, almost crazed laughter. "You heard, huh?"

Mom smiled. "Well, that's the funny thing about having a shouting match with someone outside your window. It isn't exactly private."

"What about Dad? Any chance he slept through it?"

"Oh, he tried, but I woke him up. Didn't want him to miss the show."

"Thanks," I said sarcastically.

"He's in the kitchen now, baking some cookies. Three different kinds. Drown heartbreak in calories, I always say. We can also order a pizza, if you want. I'm sure somewhere is still delivering." She gave me a big hug. "I'm sorry, hon," she whispered in my ear.

"Thanks, Mommy," I whispered back. I did feel like crying then, but I held the tears back.

"Well, I'll leave this here," Mom said, putting the ice cream on my dresser. "The cookies should be done in a few minutes. Let me know if you need anything. Love you, kids."

"Love you too, Mom Number Two," Kai said.

"I have strong feelings of affection for you as well, Mrs. O," Mel said.

With Mom gone, I turned to my best friends. "Well, who wants to play *GoldenEye*? I don't know about you guys, but I really want to just shoot a bunch of things right now. And I don't care what you say, I'm playing Oddjob. Plus, I'll be eating all this ice cream at the same time, and if you don't let me win, you're both officially the worst friends ever."

"I love you, Dylan," Mel said, "but I will never let you win."

Kai nodded. "What she said."

CHAPTER TWENTY

SO FAR it was shaping up to be a rather ordinary Tuesday. I was miserable, alone, and just generally no fun to be around. I walked in a daze from class to class. There were dozens of opportunities for jokes, wisecracks, and witty observations, but I came up blank every time. In the few weeks since my split with Adam, this had become my new, boring, depressing reality.

It was funny. Just a few months before, things were exactly like this—I was single, with no prospects for love, the only sex I was getting was from my left hand, and I spent my days bored out of my mind in school and my nights with my best friends. Yet then I was happy, and now I was categorically not. The only variable that was any different is Adam. Then we talked every day, albeit mostly yelling and insults, and now we avoided each other. It's funny that I'd miss having a bully.

I know, I know. It wasn't the bully I missed. If that really were the case, then all my problems would be solved, because a new bully had stepped up to take over Adam's old responsibilities. A new bully by the name of Will Davis who, with a sixth sense that seemed to be every asshole's gift, knew exactly how to kick me when I was down.

"It must be hard," Will was saying as we stood in the lunch line, "being the only faggot around. Lonely." I ignored him. Adam stood a few people ahead in the line. It was obvious he could hear what his supposed friend was saying, but he didn't even react.

"Oh, Will, you're not alone," Kai said. "I'm sure there's someone out there for you."

"Oh, I'm sorry, Malachi. I didn't realize it was the Jew's job to speak for the faggot."

"It's pronounced 'Fa-jay,'" Mel said. "It's French."

"Sure it is, bitch," he mumbled, turning away.

"The soul of wit, you are, Will," Mel muttered.

"Why didn't you say anything back there, Dylan?" Kai demanded when we got to our lunch table. "Normally you'd tear the guy a new one for saying even half of what he did. If it were Ad—" He gave a strangled yell and snapped his mouth shut, glaring at Mel. No doubt she had kicked him under the table. She had been becoming more and more unnecessarily protective lately. Not that I was complaining. A part of me was thankful. But the truth was, I didn't care if Kai said Adam's name. I wasn't gonna burst into tears or plunge back into the depths of sadness.

You kind of need to be happy first, before you can plunge back into anything.

Besides, he had a point. Normally I would leap at the opportunity to put an annoying jock in his place. Sure, Adam was my main sparring partner, but I'd shut down Will Davis nearly as many times, though mostly because he was right there behind Adam. Back then there had been a sense of outrage at their idiocy, a feeling of righteousness and a joy to a well-timed quip, to seeing their faces screw up with trying to figure out what exactly you had called them. Now there was only apathy. To most things, really.

And so, like we had every day that week, the three of us ate our lunches in silence. On the bright side, my dad made cookies practically every night now. So at least it was a tasty lunch.

WHEN SCHOOL had started back up again after the New Year, one of the first things I did was seek Charlotte out to apologize. I heard a good many stories about what had happened after I left. Adam stopped being the center of those girls' attentions. Instead they began to focus more and more on each other, competing for no other reason than to win. It happened rather abruptly. One second they were vying for his attention, the next there was only screaming, crying, and throwing things. It made me realize how much effort Charlotte had gone through to avoid drama at her party—and why it was so important. I had no idea things would escalate so quickly or so drastically. Mel didn't seem surprised. She told me never to underestimate the power of teenage girls to absolutely destroy any situation.

"Just be glad none of the guys got involved," she had told me, clearly speaking from experience. "That's when things really get bad."

Sometimes she frightens me.

That night wasn't a complete waste, though. Sure, the focus of the ladies' scorn had eventually shifted from Adam, which was apparently when he was able to make his escape to come plead his case to me, but there had been more than enough opportunities to make Adam feel the pain of my ire. I still heard about it from kids in the halls of school. Mostly guys, mostly speaking in admiring tones, awed at the prowess of a man who seemed able to be the object of so many women's affections. Of course, they believed Adam was straight, expected him to have enjoyed all their attention. I knew better. Their stories gave me a sick pleasure I am a little embarrassed to admit to. Stories of girls trying to tear his clothes off, of coercing him into that darkened room upstairs—of course, in their telling, it was *he* who coerced *them*—and partaking in God-knows-what depraved sex acts. The arousal in their voices was palpable as they imagined being under a pile of vaginas and surrounded by more boobs than they could count. They never guessed that, to Adam, it would have been a kind of torture.

But the point is, I felt bad about all of this. Well, specifically the ruining Charlotte's party bit. But she was very gracious in accepting my apology. She had even invited me to a few more parties—small weekend get-togethers, more along the lines of girls' nights. I even went to one, but only 'cause I knew Tiffany wasn't going to be there.

Tiffany… she was a harder problem to solve. True to what I promised myself, I did apologize to her, though I adamantly refused to explain what I was apologizing *for*. She forgave me instantly and with a laugh. She did look really confused, but that was not exactly a feeling she was unfamiliar with, and she soon forgot about the whole encounter. As far as she was concerned, we were the best of friends. Luckily, she hadn't started to suspect that I'd been avoiding her.

See, Adam's straight-guy charade wasn't a one-night affair. It had been almost two months since the party, and he was still leading Tiffany on.

"We aren't, like, boyfriend and girlfriend, you know? But just like a boy and a girl who are friends *and really like spending time together. Besides, what does boyfriend and girlfriend even* mean, *you know? They're just labels. That's what Adam says, and he's, like, really hot so, I don't know, I just go along with it."*

Tiffany talked about him all the time.

"He's, like, top ten best guys I have ever dated, easy."

Keeping quiet about it was getting harder and harder.

"Last night we spent over an hour in his car just kissing. Most guys would push for something more, you know? But Adam is just a romantic. *He knows I'm a lady."*

It was really annoying.

"Guys, how do you know if you're in love?"

It was also a real moral quandary. I mean, she was getting lied to. And it was obvious this whole thing really meant something to her. I was basically watching a friend setting herself up for heartbreak. But what could I say without compromising Adam's secrets? 'Cause I still refused to be that guy, the one who outs someone 'cause he's angry. I talked to Charlotte about it, that night I went to her girls' night, the one Tiffany didn't go to.

"Well," Charlotte said as she mixed some cookie dough. It was surprising how many of our conversations happened over baking. Also, how much of my life had come to revolve around cookies lately. "I've been trying to tell her that Adam's not good for her as subtly as I can. Especially since I can't tell her why."

"Subtle? With Tiffany? You sure you don't wanna try, I don't know, spelling it out for her?"

Charlotte waved a reproachful finger at me, though the effect was somewhat spoiled by the fact it was covered in cookie dough. "She'll surprise you." She stuck her finger in her mouth and made a delighted sound at the taste.

"I just feel like I should be doing something too."

She shook her head, an emphatic no. "You're too mad at him. That, more than anything else, will come across to her."

I wanted to argue with her that no, I wasn't mad, but some of the other girls chose that moment to join us in the kitchen. Besides, I was pretty sure she would have seen through me. I doubted she'd buy the "I'm not mad, just disappointed" shtick. I couldn't even get myself to believe it.

Now, I know that literally everyone would probably think "Gee, Dylan, why don't you talk to Mel and Kai about this? They are your best friends." At least, those who weren't thinking "Poor Dylan, things are so hard for you right now. You're such a good guy. You don't deserve this. You deserve a hug. And a cookie." Thank you, nice people, I will have a cookie. Or six.

The truth is, I didn't quite feel like I could. To understand this, you really need to understand them. They expected me to be so *sad* about all of this. And, I mean, I was sad. But they tiptoed around the subject like someone stealing honey from a napping bear. Remember that day at lunch? When it did come up, they stared at me with these faces so steeped in pity and sympathy I only wanted to punch them. At least Charlotte still acted like I was a normal fucking person.

Plus, Kai had always been against Adam. I couldn't help but feel there was a little bit of an I-told-you-so air about him. It was probably my imagination, but there you go. And Mel… well, like I said, she kinda frightened me sometimes, especially when she got protective. I half worried that every time I talked about how I feel about Adam, she got one step closer to breaking into his house and waterboarding him until he agreed to take me back.

Not that I even wanted him back necessarily.

So I talked to Charlotte sometimes instead. But mostly I kept quiet and carried on. It was one of the worst times of my life. I had been through plenty of bad times, but this was the first time I'd really felt alone, walled off from the people around me. Probably the worst part about it was how every day felt so exactly the same as the day before, like time had stopped but no one else got the memo. The cookies helped. Some. This went on for exactly forty-seven days, a period I like to call the Great Midwinter Sadness or, alternatively, the Time of Many Cookies. Things didn't get better right after. In fact, in some ways they got worse. But at least, finally, they changed.

CHAPTER TWENTY-ONE

IT STARTED with a right turn. By all accounts that day was going to be a regular Friday in February. I woke up miserable, had cookies for breakfast, sat quietly in the back of Kai's car on the way to school, staring out the window as Mel and Kai laughed. It wasn't too cold, but not unseasonably warm. Really, there was nothing about it that would make it any different from an average day. No reason for me to vary my routine.

And yet I did.

We walked into school, and Mel and Kai immediately turned left to head to our lockers, like we did every morning. I was lagging a little behind. They didn't notice—I'd been doing that a lot lately.

I stood there and watched them go, wondering if they'd see I wasn't following. They didn't, which was odd, in hindsight. Maybe I was sick of the routine, maybe I was sick of Mel and Kai themselves, or maybe I knew, somehow, that despite today's unremarkable exterior, something big was about to happen. Whatever the reason, I turned my back on their now distant figures, about to vanish into the crowd, and walked the other way. I took a right.

Of course, this wasn't really a big deal. At the time I didn't think anything of it. But in hindsight it was remarkable. If I hadn't broken my routine, hadn't turned right instead of left, I honestly have no idea how things might have changed. Because immediately after turning right, I walked past Tiffany, standing at her locker, alone and subdued. And I stopped. I'm a little surprised that I did, looking back. But not a lot—she was my friend, after all. Usually, Tiffany was bubbly, full of laughter and energy. She was rarely ever without her group of friends—they typically traveled in a pack. She never, ever stood, frozen, holding a textbook half out of her locker and staring off into space. I watched her for well over a minute before I spoke.

"Tiffany? Are you all right?"

"What?" Her head turned toward me. It was the first I'd seen her move.

"I said, are you okay? What's up?"

She looked at the textbook in her hand, finally completing the motion of putting it in her backpack. I wondered how long she had stayed like that. "Oh, I'm fine. It's just, I was thinking."

Somehow, the idea of Tiffany simply being lost in thought was more alarming. "About what?" I asked.

"About Adam," she said. That hollowness in the pit of my stomach grew. I should have known. "He broke up with me last week."

That hollowness grew even larger, was suddenly filled with butterflies and all sorts of other winged critters engaged in sudden and very bloody war. "Oh. I'm sorry."

"Oh, I'm not upset about that. I think.... It seemed like he never really liked me. This will sound weird, but it was almost like he just felt obligated to me, somehow. Like he was doing what he thought he *should*, rather than what he wanted. Sounds crazy, right?"

All I could manage was a "Huh." Charlotte was right, Tiffany really could surprise you.

"But he was always nice to me, so I'm not mad. That's more than I can say for some of the guys I've dated. He never tried to force me to do anything I didn't want to. He was always very respectful. It's funny. Being around him kind of reminded me of hanging out with you. Weird, right?" She laughed softly, shaking her head. "He kept himself so distant, but I suppose that makes sense now. I hope he's all right."

"I'm sure he is."

"I hope so. Have you seen him today?"

"No...."

"He left so abruptly yesterday. At first I thought it was me, because he didn't want to be around me. You know, after he broke it off. But then I heard his brother had called the school, got him excused. Did you know his mom was sick?"

Suddenly all the pieces of this conversation, which had been refusing to make sense, all slid and snapped into place. She didn't seem sad for herself, but for him. Pulled out of school yesterday. *Was* sick, she said. Was. It all came crashing together.

His mom had died. And he was all alone.

"I have to go." Without waiting for Tiffany to respond, I turned and ran.

"There you are," Kai said as I made it to his locker, "We were wondering where you went."

"I need your keys," I said, a little out of breath.

"You what now?" he asked, bewildered. I didn't have time to explain. I shoved my hand in his pocket and groped around for them. "This is… intrusive…," he said but didn't stop me.

I got them. "Thanks. I love you. Bye," I called over my shoulder as I left.

"What was that about?" Kai asked, watching me go.

"Beats me," Mel said.

"Am I going to regret letting him go?"

"Probably."

I NEVER really paused to think about what I was doing. Which I'm actually glad for. If I had, maybe I would have gone back. It wasn't like I didn't have the opportunity.

Principal Hayes stopped me. "Mr. O'Connor! It's been quite some time since I've seen you."

"I know. You're very disappointed." I stepped around him and kept walking. "Worry not. I'm sure that'll change soon."

"On the contrary, I find it quite heartening that…. Where are you going, Mr. O'Connor?"

"Out."

"Mr. O'Connor, if you don't turn around this instant, I'll have no choice but to—"

I paused at the threshold long enough to give Principal Hayes my most mischievous grin. "See? Things are back to normal already." With that, I let the door slam shut, relishing the look on Hayes's face.

I felt a little less cool when I got to the parking lot and could not for the life of me find Kai's car. Turns out I'd never actually paid attention. I'd follow Kai to the car, get in, wait to get where we were going, follow Kai out. So I ran up and down the aisles, pressing the unlock button on Kai's keys until I finally saw his flashing lights. I opened the door, got in, and….

Stopped.

I was in the passenger seat. Not a big deal. Sheer force of habit, right? Not like anyone was looking to see me make a fool of myself. I got out, switched sides, put the keys in the ignition, and….

Stopped.

I had no idea how to drive a car. You turned the keys—I knew that much, so I did. It started. So far so good. Right pedal, go; left pedal, stop. Put the car in "D," for Drive, presumably…. HAH! No, wait, reverse, first. See? I got this. What could go wrong?

Steering, it turned out. Didn't hit anything, though, so I decided to log that one under "success." *Now* drive. How hard could this be? I played Mario Kart—same idea, right? I played well, I usually won, I….

Stopped. Or, braked, rather.

I thought of all the times I crashed in Mario Kart. Sure, like seventy percent of those were from being run off the road by a vengeful Kai-as-Toad, but there was a good number of just swerving out for no particular reason.

"Come on, Dylan," I whispered to myself. "You can do this. It's not like there's going to be shells thrown at you every few seconds, or banana peels scattered on the road." I didn't sound very confident, even to myself. Carefully, I put the car back into drive and slowly pulled out of the school parking lot. "Hopefully."

What followed next was a very stressful, but ultimately uneventful fifteen minutes. The hardest part was probably figuring out how to make the windshield wipers work when it started to snow. I pulled up to Adam's secret spot completely unscathed, if with significantly higher blood pressure.

Adam watched as the car jerked to a stop. He stood outside his car, key in his hand, clearly about to leave. I'd made it just in time. I turned off the car, scrambled out and, standing there face to face, all the speeches I had been frantically practicing in the car suddenly fled my brain. We just stared at each other over the hood of Kai's car.

Adam was the first to think of something to say. "How'd you know I'd be here?" His face gave no indication of how he was feeling.

"It's where you go. I figured you'd need to get out of your house, so…."

His voice was soft, almost distant. "I take it you know, then, about—" His voice clouded with emotion, and he paused. When he spoke again, he sounded calm once more. "About Mom."

I nodded.

"Why are you here?" he asked.

"I—I know things between us were… you know. But I thought you shouldn't be alone right now. So I came." His face didn't change. "I'm sorry. That was stupid of me. Selfish. I'll leave you alone." I started to get back into Kai's car.

"Wait," he said, and I did.

The silence stretched on.

"Is that Kai's car?" he finally asked.

"Yeah."

"What, did you steal it and run out here the second you heard?"

"Pretty much."

"I thought you couldn't drive."

"Oh, I can't. But I had to come."

"'Cause you were worried about me?"

I shrugged.

"Thanks," he said, and for the first time, his expression changed. He smiled. I smiled back. "Aren't you going to ask if I'm okay?" he asked.

"That's a dumb question. Of course you're not okay."

"It's what everyone else keeps asking."

"Everyone else is dumb. This isn't news," I said. He laughed, and I felt a part of me relax that had been tense for months. At the same time, we both moved forward, stepped halfway around Kai's car until we were a mere few feet apart. I ached to close the distance. I think he did too.

"I really should go," he said.

"Oh." I wasn't quite able to contain my disappointment. "Okay."

"I left pretty early," he explained. "Pete's probably all alone. I don't want him to think I just ran off, like… you know."

Like his dad. "Of course. You should probably get back."

"The funeral is tomorrow morning. It's just for family. But, um, there will be a wake in the afternoon for everyone. It's at my house." For some reason, Adam had fixed his eyes firmly on his toes.

I wasn't really sure how to respond. "Sounds nice."

"Will you come?"

"What?"

"You don't have to," he rushed to explain, still staring at the ground. "I'm not trying to guilt you. You don't have to feel obligated. I know how you feel about me…."

"I'll be there."

"You will?" He was the portrait of relief.

"Great. Well, um, I should probably go…." Before he could move, I stepped forward and threw my arms around him.

"Listen," I said, hugging him tight. "I'm here for you, okay? Whatever you need, however you need me. As long as you need me. I promise. Understand?"

"Thanks," he said, hugging me back in one brief squeeze. He pulled back. "I'll see you tomorrow, then?"

"Definitely."

Adam glanced at Kai's car. "Maybe have someone else drive you, huh?"

"Nah, it's cool. I'm a quarter crash-test dummy, on my father's side." I was graced with another smile for my efforts, though it might have seemed a little forced. Then Adam got in his car, and I waved as he drove away.

"Well," I said to Kai's car. "It's what, almost time for second period? Guess I might as well get that detention out of the way." I climbed back into the car, this time remembering to sit in the driver's seat. "Wait, how does this thing work again?"

CHAPTER TWENTY-TWO

THIS WAS the first time I'd ever been to Adam's house. It was a small, two-story building nestled in the woods near the edge of town. It was absolutely packed with people. I had been a little nervous before I came. What if the entire football team was there, and I spent, like, an hour cornered by Will Davis? But when I got there, all I could see were adults standing around in too nice clothes, eating off small paper plates and talking solemnly amongst themselves, and small kids running around, ignoring their parents' pleas to behave and not dirty their brand-new clothes.

I wasn't sure whether I should ring the doorbell or come right in. I saw a bunch of people going in and out the front door, so I assumed the latter. A number of men stood on the front porch, smoking. They were old men, mostly overweight, with large unkempt beards and ill-fitting suits. It was pretty warm for February, but I was still surprised that none of them wore jackets. I had this sense that the only jackets they owned were ratty old things, which had been forbidden by wives who had also forced them into the suits they had worn when they were much thinner men. I assumed they were friends of Adam's father, though I didn't see him among them. They made me nervous in that way groups of old men with that air of conservative masculinity had always made me feel. I was very self-conscious of my neat new suit, my polished shoes and styled hair. After all, these were probably the kind of men Adam had grown up around, grown up feeling like he could never come out.

They nodded to me as I stepped onto the porch, a respectful hello. One of them held the door open for me. Honestly, I was a little surprised they didn't turn me away, tell me to leave like they could sense the gayness rolling off me.

Maybe I was being unfair.

I found Adam toward the back of the living room. I waited as he talked with two old—bordering on ancient—women. He noticed me as I got closer. He spared me a quick smile, but then turned back to his conversation with, I'm guessing, his great-aunts.

They did most of the talking. Mostly comments on how short life is, how unfair, taken too young, etc., all interspersed with *tsk*ing noises and ponderously shaken heads. Adam barely got a word in edgewise. It was obvious that, despite being the one who'd just lost a mother, *he* was the one doing most of the comforting today.

The little old ladies finished, and I finally had my chance to talk to Adam.

"You look nice," he said as I stepped up.

"Thanks. You do too." He really did. Dark suit, a tie. He cut a really dashing figure. It was a shame he didn't dress like this more often. "I, uh, brought a casserole. 'Cause apparently that's what you do."

"Thanks. You can set it over there with all the others." He pointed to a table already laden with food. I saw at least four other casserole dishes, as well as a few cakes, several plates of cookies, and what looked to be an entire turkey. Apparently the idea that sadness could be somehow mitigated with food was universal.

We stood there awkwardly for a moment. At least, *I* felt awkward. It was a little hard to tell what Adam was feeling. I'd never really interacted with him before in public, so I was kind of at a loss as to what I could say. I probably couldn't give him a hug in front of everyone. I mean, I'd noticed a good amount of interguy hugging in there already, but that was clearly more platonic, "we're obviously cousins or something" kind of hugging. I couldn't shake the probably irrational fear that everyone would notice the gayness radiating off any overt affection coming from me.

"Listen," Adam eventually said. "I should probably mingle with my family. Almost all of them are here from out of state."

"Yeah, totally. I'll just set this down with the others," I said, indicating the casserole. "I guess."

Adam reached out and gave my arm a tiny squeeze, then stepped away to talk with some guy holding a baby. I was a little ashamed that *he* was the one giving *me* a reassuring arm touch. Good God, I was terrible at this.

Not knowing what else to do, I set my casserole with all the others, snuck a cookie from one of the opened cookie tins (okay, it was like nine, don't judge me, I was stressed) and started walking around Adam's house. People who I passed gave me restrained smiles and polite hellos. None of them seemed to care who I was, or why I was there. Looking around, I noticed several other people—usually in couples, but sometimes alone—who also didn't seem to know anyone else there. People who showed up to pay their own respects for a neighbor, or a coworker, or something. Noticing this made me feel a little more comfortable. A little more anonymous.

In the hallway by the stairs, I found a row of pictures. Many of them were of Adam and his brother Pete throughout the years, two little blond boys roughhousing, grinning at the camera, or posing with various sports equipment. It was a very weird experience for me. I remembered Adam at all of these ages, but in my memories he was usually sneering, this imposing figure who always loomed over me and terrorized me. Even after everything that had happened between us, I realized I had still held on to this image of him—of us—as kids.

In reality, he had been a small kid, cute, and often overshadowed by his older brother. In one picture, he was trapped in a headlock, though he smiled. In another, his brother stood holding a new toy on Christmas morning, while little Adam sat on the floor amid the wrapping paper, waiting his turn. In many he stood right behind, always letting Pete be the focus, almost like he was trying to hide. He looked out of those pictures with a sadness I knew all too well—the sadness of knowing you're different, and trying not to show it.

Eventually, the pictures began to show Adam as he was now. That sadness seemed to lessen with each passing year, but I knew better. He'd merely gotten better at hiding it. His smiles started to seem more genuine, and he rarely stood in his brother's shadow. But I knew that, inside, he was still that sad little kid. I knew it, 'cause he had shown it to me, in those times we were alone. I realized that, without me, he probably didn't show it to anyone.

Then there were the pictures of his mom.

This was the first time I'd seen her. She was a small woman, very thin and very blond. She was practically dwarfed by her children, but despite that, she seemed to dominate the picture. She had an aura of warmth that I could almost feel through the frame. Her smile made her glow, and I recognized it instantly. It was the same smile I'd seen on Adam's face those times when he'd been truly, happily carefree. Those few times we had been alone together.

In fact, the more I looked, the more I could see how much Adam looked like his mother. Pete, on the other hand, clearly took much more after their father. His hair had grown darker after puberty, and he sported an almost identically square chin. I couldn't find very many pictures of Adam's dad to make some more comparisons. There didn't appear to be any of him, outside of the few with the whole family. There were a few lighter spots on the wall, where it looked like pictures had once hung. I wondered what they had been of, why they had been taken down.

Short of going upstairs, I ran out of house to explore. So I watched Adam as he moved effortlessly from person to person throughout the room. Each time I couldn't shake the sensation that he was the one doing the comforting, never receiving comfort. He radiated strength, even warmth, that I could now recognize as coming from his mom. He was clearly trying, with all his heart, to be like her today. In his attitude, I saw that sad little boy, spending years imitating his mother, only now he was forced to go on without example. I doubt anyone else noticed. He made it seem so effortless.

A few times, I saw Pete across the room. I remembered Pete from school, and though he had graduated two years ago, he might have recognized me. He might have questioned why I was there when no one else from school was. Not only that, there had been quite a stir when I came out, the only kid at Oak Lake to do so in memory. It would be even worse if he not only recognized me as a kid from school, but as *that fag* Adam had bullied for all those years. Best-case scenario, he would think I was there to gloat at my bully's pain. Worst case, he would guess the truth. So I played it safe and kept groups of people between us whenever possible. There were a few times when I could almost swear he was looking across the room, right at me. But most of the time, he was gone, somewhere or other, leaving Adam alone to mingle with all the guests.

The day passed. I didn't get another chance to talk with Adam. He never had a spare moment. Occasionally I'd notice him frantically scanning the crowd, looking like the facade he had so carefully crafted was about to slip. His eyes would find mine, he'd smile and turn back to his conversation. It was like knowing I was there gave him the strength to continue, or at least that he didn't want me to leave.

Eventually, as night fell, the crowd thinned as people started to leave. I finally got to sit on the big armchair in the living room. I'd been eyeing it for the last two hours, but it hadn't been unoccupied until now. I sat and watched as Adam consoled his aunt.

Adam's glances in my direction became more and more frequent, until barely a minute passed between them. It was obvious he wanted to come over to me, but he never did. One by one, the remaining guests interrupted their conversation to give Adam their good-byes. His aunt barely paused in her monologue of grief each time, and soon she was the last one there—except for me, of course. Adam remained dutifully attentive throughout. Pete was nowhere to be seen.

After what felt like another hour, Adam's aunt finally finished, and he walked her out. A minute later, her headlights disappeared down the driveway and Adam stepped back inside. We were finally alone.

The mask of strength was gone. Adam looked exhausted. He collapsed, eyes closed, onto the couch across from me.

I stood up and looked around, half expecting Pete to show up, but we were truly alone. I sat at the opposite end of the couch. I listened hard and heard only the sound of Adam's breathing. I scooted over until I was sitting next to him. Adam's head dropped on my shoulder. His breathing deepened. I began to fret that he had fallen asleep, that Pete would barge in any second.

Adam's fingers brushed mine. I looked down at him, but he still gave no sign that he was anything but asleep. I struggled to be half as relaxed.

"Aren't you afraid Pete will see us?" I asked softly.

Adam's eyes snapped open, and he lifted his head. "Do you see Pete anywhere?" He stood up, crossed the room, and grabbed a picture frame off the bookshelf. I'd looked at that picture earlier in the day. It was a picture of Adam and Pete, when Adam was around ten years old, sitting on their mom's lap.

"Adam?" I asked. "What is it?"

He didn't look up from the picture. "Will you stay tonight? I don't want to be alone."

Immediately, my stomach clenched. *Say no, oh God, say no,* said the part of me still hurting from his betrayal. *He's only looking for some life-affirming comfort sex.* It had a point. "Of course," I said instead. The look of relief on his face was immediate.

Fuck, I thought, *I hope I don't regret this.*

CHAPTER TWENTY-THREE

HE LED me upstairs to his room. He started changing out of his nice suit. I didn't quite feel comfortable with watching, so I occupied myself with exploring his room. It was extraordinarily clean. Not even a few abandoned pieces of clothing on the floor. His suit immediately went on hangers, and his used undershirt into a small hamper hidden in his closet. It seemed almost clinical.

The walls were a very plain off-white with no posters anywhere. The furniture was unremarkable, the bedding plain. The desk was the only place in the room that felt at all lived-in, with its scattered homework assignments and textbooks. His trophies were lined on the back of the desk, and also along the windowsill. There were over a dozen of them, across several different sports and ages. They must have represented his entire life's achievements, at least those he wanted to remember and display. But what caught my eye most, perhaps because it was the only color in the room, outside of the burnished gold of the trophies, was a stained glass pendant, about the size of a small cell phone, hanging by a ribbon from one of the trophies on the windowsill. It was beautiful, deep blues, brilliant reds and greens forming no particular pattern, becoming instead a sort of calming chaos. From the way it was hanging, I could tell that, had it been day, it would have caught the light perfectly from the window.

"What's this?" I asked, reaching out to take hold of the pendant.

Adam came up behind me, dressed now in the plain T-shirt and sweatpants I was used to. "It was for you. I was going to give it to you for Christmas, but I never got the chance." I was speechless. But even if I hadn't been, Adam didn't give me the opportunity to respond. "Here, you can wear these," he said, handing me a neatly folded pair of sweatpants, a T-shirt, and even a clothes hanger for the suit I was wearing.

I took them from him. "Thanks. I'll just—" But he had already stepped out of the room. I stared at the shut door for a second after he left. Had he left to give me privacy? Or was there something else going on? Either way, I was going to take advantage of it to change. Sure, Adam had seen me naked, but that was *before*. I was grateful for the privacy.

Adam's clothes were pretty baggy on me. Luckily the sweatpants had a drawstring, or I'd have had to hold them up with one hand throughout the night. I finished changing, hung my suit neatly on the clothes hanger I'd been given, but Adam still hadn't returned. So I took the opportunity to send my parents a text.

I won't be home tonight.

I hesitated sending it. How honest should I be?

Spending the night at Kai's.

My mom responded almost immediately. *Uh-huh. Sure you are.*

Dad's reply came right after. *Does this mean I'm not gonna have to make cookies every night from now on? 'Cause your mom's gonna be disappointed.*

I rolled my eyes and didn't respond.

The door opened. "I found a toothbrush for you, if you want." Adam tossed me an unopened toothbrush.

"Thanks," I said and followed him to the bathroom.

We brushed our teeth, side by side and in silence. I watched Adam in the mirror, gave him sidelong glances, but he kept his eyes firmly fixed on the sink. I started to get annoyed. Why was I even here? I was being ignored so thoroughly, it was almost as if I weren't. We brushed in silence, finished in silence, walked back to Adam's room in silence. Adam lay down on his bed—you guessed it—in silence. He rolled over, putting his back to me.

Well, here it comes, I thought, looking down at him in the darkness. *The "comforting."* I wasn't sure I was okay with this. I was still upset with him. It was one thing to put that aside, for now, but being a grief-fuck was quite another. *Come on, Dylan, his mom just died. He needs you to be there for him.* Yeah, but I wasn't planning on being quite as "there" as this. *What would you regret more, a quick comfort fuck or abandoning someone you care about, whether you want to admit it or not, to deal with his grief alone?*

Fuck.

So I lay down too, crawled under the covers, and tried to force my trepidation aside.

Adam immediately rolled toward me, put his arm around my waist and his head on my chest. *Okay, not what I was expecting.* Awkwardly, I placed my arm on his back, gave him a little pat. After a minute, I felt a wetness seep through my shirt.

He's crying, I realized. Not sobbing—he was making no noise, only shedding silent tears. Weeping, I guess, would be the word to use here. I had never seen anyone weep before. When Kai's dad died, he had sobbed for days. Granted, that was Kai, and we were twelve, but Adam wasn't sobbing. I think I assumed he was… not okay, obviously but… I don't really know. Suddenly, I realized Adam hadn't been ignoring me before. He'd just been sad and probably felt like he couldn't let it out until we were alone. In the dark. That's probably also why he avoided me all day, because he didn't want his composure to slip. I was right that he needed comforting, but I didn't expect it to be, well, literal comforting. Holy fuck, I'm an idiot.

I didn't say anything. I just brushed his hair with my fingers until we fell asleep.

I WOKE up with an intense thirst. The clock on Adam's bedside table read 1:00 a.m. in harsh red light. Sometime while we slept, Adam had rolled off me, and now he lay at the far side of the bed. I slipped out of bed, careful not to wake him up, and made my way downstairs to the kitchen to grab a drink of water.

The house was still. I self-consciously glanced at the hallway leading to the stairs to the basement, where I knew Pete's bedroom was. It was silent, but I could see the faint glow of a light left on. I tried my best to locate a glass in silence, but was continually thwarted by the kitchen's propensity for noises. Stepped on the wrong part of the floor, creak. Opened a cupboard too quickly, squeak. Opened a cupboard too slowly, groan. I half expected the refrigerator to start singing, just to spite me. Eventually I found a cup—a mug, but at that point I wasn't about to be picky—and filled it with water. Noisy faucets. Surprise, surprise.

"Who the fuck are you?" I heard slurred behind me.

I turned around. Looming in the doorway, silhouetted by the light from the hall, was Pete. He still wore his ill-fitting suit, though it was unbuttoned and extremely wrinkled. Even across the room, I could smell the alcohol on him. He was enormous, intimidating, and radiating menace.

With as much dignity as I could muster, I cowered. "I'm Adam's friend."

Pete stepped closer. "You're that faggot, aren't you?"

He seemed to expect some response. "Um…."

"What the fuck are you doing here, faggot?"

He was getting really close. "Adam asked me to stay," I said.

"You're disgusting," he continued, not seeming to have heard me. "You're trying to convert him, aren't you? Exploiting his grief so you can have your way with him."

"What? No, it's not like that at all," I said. Pete snarled and shoved me, hard. My back hit the pantry with a loud thud. Pain shot up my spine, and I collapsed to the floor. Pete stared down at me, hands balled into fists.

"I won't let you take advantage of him," he shouted.

I wanted to close my eyes, but I couldn't stop staring at his fist as he raised it to strike.

CHAPTER TWENTY-FOUR

IN AN instant, Adam was there. He grabbed Pete's arm.

"You will not touch him." Adam didn't yell, or even sound particularly angry. Instead, his voice was soft and almost dangerous. "It's one thing to hit me. I'm your little brother. I'm supposed to get beat up every now and again. That's all well and good. But I will not stand by and watch you hurt the guy I love—"

Wut.

"—because you are too big of a coward to deal with what you're feeling. Just like Dad. Well, I can act like Dad too. If you so much as look at him wrong again, I'll leave. And I'll never come back." With that, he pushed Pete's arm away. He didn't use all that much force, but in Pete's inebriated state, it was enough to send him stumbling and land flat on his ass.

Pete stared up at his brother, mouth moving wordlessly as his booze-addled mind was reeling for purchase. In that instant, I finally saw him as he really was. He wasn't this aggressive older brother to be feared, a tyrant, pillar of imposing strength. He was just a person—a kid, really—already developing a beer belly from drinking, probably by himself more often than not, hair thinning way too early. One can only hope that isn't in Adam's future, but I digress. A guy whose mom had just died and who was trying desperately to be the adult he suddenly needed to be, but without any example other than a drunk, sometimes abusive father who ran away. A guy who was too weak to do any better. Though, in his situation, it's hard to believe that very many people would. In that moment, I pitied him.

Ha, that's a lie. I mean, I'm awesome and smarter than, like, everyone else, but not even I'm that perceptive on the fly. It was actually about three days later while telling this story to Kai that I made this realization.

In reality, and this seriously is the last time I'll admit this, as I lay on the floor (okay, cowered, really. Classy, I know), all I could do was look up at Adam standing protectively over me, hands balled into fists, his broad, muscled shoulders tensed with anger—to be honest, like, 95 percent of my memories of this moment are Adam-muscle-related—and swoon. A mini, I'm-already-on-the-floor-type swoon, but a swoon nonetheless. In my imagination, my suddenly adrenaline- and pain-enhanced imagination, he was suffused with a halo of righteous wrath, an aura of hero that seemed plucked straight from a fairy tale. I knew the whole damsel-in-distress thing was really not a good look, but that was where I was at. It didn't help matters when a second later he turned and scooped me up in his arms and carried me upstairs. The only thing that could have cemented my damsel status any further was if I were being carried from a tower or some shit. It was magical. It made my stomach tingle in that "someone fulfilled my secret wish and I won't ever even have to admit I liked it" kind of way.

But for the sake of my ego, let's pretend I picked myself up, told Adam that Pete wasn't worth it—or maybe something compassionate instead—and walked upstairs myself in a dignified, manly manner, because I am the hero of this story. Definitely not the damsel. If anyone was the damsel, it was… well, not Adam, certainly. Far too many muscles there. But someone else, someone not me. Kai, probably.

Heh. Yeah, it was definitely Kai.

Where was I?

Oh yes. Back in Adam's room, in his bed—I was *not* placed there by Adam's big, strong arms, how dare you even think it? I walked, remember?—I expected Adam to pace back and forth, quivering with pent-up energy, or something, especially after how he had acted downstairs. But he didn't. He stood there, slouched against the door, eyes closed. He looked exhausted. He looked defeated, though I can't imagine why. It seemed to me like he had won a victory against his brother. He looked, well, vulnerable.

I said before that the sight of him naked captured my heart. This was only partially true. It was seeing him vulnerable that really did it. He showed me the scared little boy he hid deep inside. The naked only let my cock catch up to what my heart had already begun to realize. And now, seeing him like this, my brain started to catch up too.

"Did you mean it?"

He opened his eyes and looked weakly at me. "Mean what?"

"That you love me."

His eyes closed again. He slid down the door until he was sitting on the floor, knees hugged tight to his chest. He buried his face in his arms and shrugged.

"Oh," I said. Not my best. I wasn't exactly feeling quick on my feet at the moment.

"I know," he said, "I ruined it. The only good thing I've ever had, and I wrecked it." He looked up at me. Tears were streaming down his face, but his voice was steady. "And now I've lost you. I know it. I'm not trying to…." He paused, clearly struggling for words. He gave up and dropped his head again.

"Adam," I said. I slid off the bed and laid my hand on his arm. He met my eyes. "Don't worry. I'm here now. I told you, I'm here as long as you need me."

"But what about a month from now? How about two? When you stop feeling bad for me, what then?"

"I…." I was taken aback by the intensity of his gaze. I didn't know how to respond.

"You'll leave again, and I'll go back to being alone."

"Adam, I… I'm not okay with being your secret anymore, with hiding from the rest of the school. I just…."

Adam cut me off. "Shit, I told my *brother*, and you think I'm worried about the school?" He sighed and looked away. "I'm sorry. I didn't mean to—you know. I'm aware it's my fault. I'm not trying to make you feel guilty. You have every right to…. It's just…. Maybe you should just go. It will hurt less later if you went now." He stood up and walked across the room, very deliberately putting his back to me.

I stood up too. "Fuck it."

"What?" he said, confused.

"I said fuck it. You think you were the only one upset about this, the only one who feels lonely? It would be easier for me to count the nights I *haven't* cried myself to sleep, and most of those were because I just straight up wasn't able to sleep at all. I've missed you, every day. You're right. It is all your fault. I do have the right to… to cut you out of my life, or make you pay, or whatever you were about to say. Instead, I say fuck it."

He turned back toward me. "What are you saying?" he asked, trepidation in his voice.

"Fuck it. I think we've covered that part."

"Dylan, please don't make jokes right now."

"I'm saying that I don't know if I love you, but this is the closest to love I think I've ever felt. I'm saying that I don't want you to not be a part of my life. I'm saying can't we just skip the part with the reconciling and the forgiveness-seeking? I'm saying why aren't you over here kissing me, right now? I'm saying—"

I never had a chance to finish saying what it was I was saying. 'Cause right then I was hit by about two hundred pounds of muscle, and my mouth suddenly became quite occupied with other pursuits. Like trying to find time for breaths between kisses.

"You didn't let me finish," I said, once the bout of making out came to a close, with my back against the door and our foreheads pressed together.

"Oh?" Adam said softly. "It couldn't have been too important."

"I wouldn't be too sure about that."

"What was it, then?"

"Remember how I was saying fuck it?"

"Vaguely."

"Well, I kinda meant that literally too."

Adam's face slowly morphed into a wicked, hungry grin. He picked me up, I wrapped my legs around his waist, and he carried me to his bed. We were making out pretty heavily at this point. He dropped me on the bed and tore my pants off with one hand. Only then did he stop kissing me. I had a second to gasp for air before he took my cock in his mouth, deep-throating me with reckless abandon, and making me lose my breath all over again. I pulled his shirt up over his head. He hesitated to stop sucking me long enough to get his shirt off. I had to tug on it a few times before he let me get it off. I pulled his head up to kiss me again, and he ripped my shirt off—*not* a figure of speech, by the way, which made me glad it was *his* shirt. I reached down and freed his cock, already swollen and massive, from his pants. It was bliss to hold him in my hand again. But it wasn't enough.

"Fuck me, Adam. I want you to fuck me!"

As if by magic, Adam made condoms and lube appear. Seriously, he could have pulled them from behind my ear for all I could tell. To this day, I still wonder if he'd had them in his pocket the whole time, or stashed under the pillow for such an emergency. Still kissing me, he squeezed some lube onto his fingers and began to rub it around my asshole. He slipped one finger in, then two, working in and out, widening my hole. I gasped with each penetration, as though surprised every time, and he laughed between kisses. Then he tore open the condom, put it on, and positioned himself, cock pressed against me. I looked up at him. He looked down at me.

And then he was inside me.

For an instant, it was uncomfortable. So tight, not painful, but like my body was resisting an intrusion. Then he pulled out halfway, thrust back in, and my back arched in pleasure. He did it, again and again, and with each thrust I could feel his cock rubbing against my insides—my prostate, said a small part of my brain, but I was much too far gone to listen—sending waves of sensation through my body until my toes curled and I cried out uncontrollably. Faster he went, and harder, until I thought I would go blind from the ecstasy. He grabbed my cock and stroked in time with his thrusts, while bending down to kiss me. He grabbed my hips to pull me against him and add more power to his thrusts. I wanted it to never end.

But it did, and way too soon. He called out my name as he came. He collapsed on the bed beside me and gazed at me with heavy lidded eyes.

He tore open another condom, rolled it on my cock with a deft motion, and said, "Now it's my turn." Whatever small disappointment I might have felt vanished, replaced with lust.

I started with one finger, listening to him moan. When I switched to two, he was writhing beneath me, begging for more. By the time I pressed my cock against his taut hole, he was hard again, and his eyes burned with desire.

"Fuck me," he moaned. And I did. "Harder," he begged, and I obliged. With each thrust, I plunged my cock deep into him, shoving him hard against the mattress. He cried out with each thrust, louder and louder, and before long I was too, shouting in unison. I grabbed his cock and pumped it in counterpoint with each of my thrusts until, shuddering, we both came. I collapsed onto his chest. We lay there, for several minutes, panting, my slowly softening cock still inside him.

"God, I missed that." Adam pushed me gently off him. He pulled a small towel from a drawer on his bedside table, wiped the cum off his chest, then pulled the condom off me and cleaned me up. "Don't get me wrong. I missed you too…."

"Uh-huh," I said lazily, "Sure. And what was it, exactly, you missed about me?"

"Okay, you got me. I only missed the fucking." We both laughed. It felt good to be so carefree again. It had been so long.

"Can I ask you a question?"

"Shoot." Adam said.

"What made you change your mind? About all this?"

"I couldn't resist the call of your manly allure any longer," Adam joked.

"I mean, it is pretty overpowering. But seriously. I know you broke it off with Tiffany over a week ago. Why?"

Adam's smile faded, and that look of saddened introspection crept back. He sat up, leaned against the headboard with a faraway look in his eyes. Seeing the complete change in his demeanor, I regretted bringing it up. I was about to apologize, say never mind, when he started talking.

"You skipped a question. Why did I do it in the first place?"

I tried to be reassuring. "I know why. You don't have to—"

"I don't think you do." He took a deep breath. "My dad came home, on Christmas."

Not what I was expecting. "Oh," I said, because I'm always so good at knowing what to say.

"Pete and I got home from visiting Mom, and there he was. Really drunk. His friend was there, waiting with Dad. Said he didn't know where else to take him." Adam smiled bitterly, nearly a grimace.

"Apparently Dad's run away from everyone, not just us. He… said some things. A lot of things, really. One thing he kept going on about was whose fault it was. The cancer. Who he blamed. Doctors. God. Himself. Me and Pete. I don't know if he really blamed us the most, but that's what sticks in my memory. I can't stop seeing him, standing there with that look on his face…." Adam cleared his throat. "I remember that night, laying here, I kept thinking, he's right, but not for the reasons he was saying. It was my fault. We were being punished because of me, because I was… with you."

Holy shit. "Adam, of course it's not—"

"Please." He cut me off. "Just… don't. I know it's not my fault. Obviously. But it's what I felt then. I wish you would stop dismissing my struggles because you think they're easy."

"I…." I don't do that, is what I had been about to say. But before I could even finish the sentence, our entire relationship flashed before my eyes. I saw myself behaving like I always had to reassure him, hold his hand, and lead him down the path to gayness. I had been trying to help, to be understanding. I realized how it must have felt, to have someone continually saying "I know why you're scared. I was there once. But don't worry, one day you'll catch up to me!" But mostly I remembered New Year's Eve, and the overpowering need I had felt to act superior. Condescending.

"I'm sorry," I said instead. "I don't mean to."

"I know. It's okay. I mean, you're stupid and I hate you, but that's not new."

"Oh yeah. We covered that way back in the third grade." We grinned at each other. A small bit of that carefree atmosphere seeped back in, so naturally I had to immediately go and ruin it. "So what happened?"

"I tried to be straight."

I rolled my eyes. "I know that, dumbass. I was there for that part. I meant, why did you stop?"

"I know," he said with a sigh. "I just didn't really want to talk about it."

"I'm sorry. You don't have to."

"No, I want to." He fell silent. I waited for him to continue.

"I visit her almost every day." He winced. "Visited, I mean. Usually, Pete wouldn't come. She would ask what was bothering me. You didn't really know her, but she had this way about her sometimes. Like she already knew everything, but was waiting for everyone else to realize it. So when she asked, I kept feeling like she was expecting something specific. But I'd always say it was nothing. Or I'd tell her about school. Something. She always accepted my answer, believed it, but the next day she'd say the exact same thing, in the exact same way, like she hadn't quite gotten the answer she wanted yet. I'm not dumb—I think a part of me knew what she was driving at. I guess I was scared or couldn't admit that I hadn't hidden it as well as I thought, or something. Then one day I realized that she—" He took a deep, steadying breath before continuing. "That she might die, and I'd never have the chance to tell her. That I was letting fear take my choice away. I started to think that she was holding on, just for me, to give me that chance. The doctors had been saying since January that any day could be her last. But every day, there she was, asking what was bothering me.

"Then one day, when she asked, the words just bubbled up. 'I think I might be in love,' I said. And she said 'yes.' Not, like, 'oh yeah?' like it was a question, or she was confused. Only 'yes.' Like I had finally said what she wanted to hear. 'With a boy,' I said. I was still scared, but I had already started. I knew I had to say it. And she said 'Good.' She smiled at me, made me promise I would be happy. Suddenly I didn't want to pretend anymore. The next day, I broke up with Tiffany. A week later, Mom was gone." He surreptitiously wiped away his tears with the heel of his hand, looking annoyed at his own display of emotion. "And that's how it happened." He looked down at me, his naked body bathed in moonlight from the window, and saw something in my face. "What?"

"I love you." It surprised me. Not that I said it, exactly. I had felt it coming. But by how much I meant it. It made me kind of nervous. "I just realized that I hadn't told you. That I've never told you how much I care about you actually. 'Cause I do. Care about you, I mean." I clamped my mouth shut before I babbled myself to death.

Adam smiled. "I know," he said.

"Really? Is that all you've got to say? No 'I love you too'? Typical."

"I already said it!"

"Actually, what you said was more like 'I love *him*.' You didn't even say it to me."

"Oh, same thing."

"Plus it was in the heat of the moment, so it doesn't count."

"Seriously?"

"How am I supposed to know it wasn't just the excitement talking?"

"Fine. Dylan O'Connor, I love you."

"You were clearly only saying that 'cause I coerced you…."

He growled and grabbed me. I yelped and tried to roll away. We wrestled, laughing, until before long he was on top of me, pinning me down. Then he kissed me.

"I love you, you stupid fairy," he said.

"I love you, you fucking jock."

"Do we really have to fight, even about loving each other?" he asked with a smile.

"Wouldn't be fun otherwise, now would it?"

"I suppose not."

CHAPTER TWENTY-FIVE

THE NEXT morning I discovered that Adam's bedroom had east-facing windows, and that he had hung the stained glass pendant perfectly so that the morning sun shone through it. I awoke, wrapped in the arms of the man I love, bathed in scintillating, multicolored light. It was perfect.

Of course, it was quickly ruined by the same scourge that plagues every lazy morning, an urgent bladder nagging for relief. I ignored it, luxuriated in the moment for as long as I could, until I hit the point of diminishing returns where the scales finally tipped in the direction of discomfort. Even so, I put off getting up for another few minutes, until I couldn't stand it anymore and had to get up.

Adam had other ideas. "Nope," he said as I tried to slip out of his arms. He pulled me back against him, snuggled in, and promptly fell back asleep. I couldn't exactly be mad—I hadn't wanted to get up in the first place. After a minute, I tried again but couldn't make his arms budge.

"You're not really asleep, are you?" In response, Adam began to snore loudly. He was obviously faking. "Come on. I really have to pee."

Adam thrust his hips slowly forward, rubbing his hard cock against my ass. "Me too," he said.

"I thought you were asleep," I said sarcastically.

"Mmm," he replied, thrusting again. He reached around and grabbed my cock, stiff with morning wood.

"Yeah, as much as I appreciate this—and don't get me wrong, I really do—anything that comes out of there will, best-case scenario, be only one part cum for every three parts piss. As much as I'm sure watersports are fine and dandy," I said sarcastically, "maybe your bed isn't the best place to test that one out."

"Watersports? What's that?"

I flipped around to face him, see if he was serious. Apparently he was. "You're gonna have to use context clues to figure that one out, bub."

"Ew, people really do that?"

"Yup. It's certainly a strange one. Have you never watched Internet porn?"

"No. I've always been too afraid someone would catch me, or find the browser history."

"Well, you're about fifteen seconds from experiencing it firsthand, unless you let me get up."

"Fine." Adam kissed me. "I suppose—" Another kiss. "—I could be convinced—" Kiss. "—to let you go. But I'm—" Couple of kisses that time. "Coming with you." He finally let me go, and we both climbed out of bed.

Adam unselfconsciously strode straight out of his room without bothering to get dressed. I was a little more nervous, poking my head out the door and looking both ways before sprinting after him, cupping my junk in my hands. I mean, I was barely comfortable walking around my own house naked unless I was absolutely sure no one was home. Even then I felt kinda weird about it. And there was a distinct lack of a violently homophobic brother at my house.

The morning bathroom ritual was more silly than sexy. We both peed at the same time, giggling, which made me feel particularly silly. Toothbrushing was punctuated with a good deal of elbowing and snide-comment-making. The being-naked part just made the whole thing that much more fun. Besides, this was the first time I'd been able to just be around a naked Adam for such a long time. Sure, there'd been a good amount of nakedness before, but we were mostly pretty occupied at the time. There was a definite appeal to being able to watch him be casually naked, admire his body in its entirety. Of course, there was only so much of that one could take until one's body began to notice and perked up with interest. So we fumbled our way back to the bedroom to take care of that before heading downstairs.

Getting dressed proved to be an equal disappointment for us both. It was still kind of weird to think that Adam got as much pleasure from watching my body as I did his, but that was apparently the case. It was only my body. It wasn't even that special. But when I put on pants, he complained far more loudly than I did when he dressed. Quite the ego boost. I found myself laughing, almost uncontrollably, out of sheer happiness. Adam laughed too.

The laughter cut off when we walked in the kitchen. Pete was there, standing in front of the stove, preparing something. He acknowledged our presence with a quick glance and a nod, turned right back to his cooking. He poked at something in the skillet, an unconvincing attempt at seeming busy. I looked at Adam with an expression that was part "now what," part "holy shitfuck run away!" He shrugged, sat down at the table. I followed suit. Cautiously.

To my surprise, it was Pete who broke the silence. "How many pancakes do you want?"

Adam looked from Pete to me and back. Clearly, he had no idea what to expect. This conversation was completely uncharted waters for us both. It was possibly much more frightening to him, though if it was, he didn't show it.

"Um, two for me, I guess."

"What about—" Pete hesitated. "I don't actually know his name."

"Dylan," I introduced myself. "And I'll have, like, six at least. I'm not a pussy, like some people."

Pete laughed, a sort of awkward, taken-off-guard kind of laugh. It cut off kind of abruptly, and he self-consciously cleared his throat. "I'm, uh, really sorry about last night. I was totally out of line." I thought Adam's eyes were gonna pop right out of his head, he looked so shocked. "It's just, I was a real mess last night. Everyone being there had set me on edge. I had too much to drink. Dad never showed up, not that I even expected him to…." He trailed off, cleared his throat again. Emotion had clearly overwhelmed him, and desperate not to let it show, he had no idea how to continue.

Incongruously, Adam looked to me, wide-eyed, as though for guidance. I inclined my head toward Pete, pulling my best "get your ass over there and comfort your brother, stupid" face. *Me?* he mouthed. *Yes, you,* I mouthed back. *Why me?* I gave him a flat stare until he finally got up and stepped across the kitchen.

Adam hesitantly placed his hand on his brother's shoulder. "Dad's an asshole," he said.

Pete gave a mirthless laugh. The two looked at each other in some silent solidarity before clearing their throats nearly in unison and stepping away from each other. It was the weirdest display I had ever witnessed, especially because they were both so clearly uncomfortable as though they had somehow gotten *too* emotional.

"So you two are, um, together?" Pete asked, sounding like he was trying at nonchalance but failed in the follow-through.

Adam tensed visibly. "There a problem with that?"

"What? No, dude. I mean, fuck. Yes, it weirds me out a little. But you're my baby brother, I don't want to be shut out of your life. If you want to be gay, I won't try and stop you."

"It's not really a question of want, Pete."

"Fuck, dude, you know what I meant."

"I do. And thank you. I was really worried you wouldn't…." Adam trailed off.

"What, love you anymore? Naw, dude, fuck that. What gave you that stupid idea?"

"Seriously? You've always been such an asshole, maybe not as bad as last night, but—"

"Well, maybe if you had told me earlier I'd have known better than to be such an asshole—"

"Maybe if you hadn't been such an asshole, I'd have actually felt like I could tell you—"

"If you weren't such a pussy—"

"Douchebag."

"Nerd."

"Idiot."

"Gay nerd."

And suddenly the two were laughing. This had the feel of an old ritual, sibling bickering that had gone on so long it had become nostalgic. The two of them hugged then, a quick backslapping affair. Then Pete turned back to the pancakes, and Adam sat back down by me.

"Dylan," he whispered, "are you crying?"

"What? Acceptance makes me emotional. Shut up."

Adam grinned a big dopey grin. "Yeah, that was pretty cool."

The pancakes were done, and we all ate together. If Pete was at all uncomfortable around me, he gave no sign. Indeed, the three of us laughed and joked, and had an all-around great breakfast. And when Adam reached out and held my hand, on *top* of the table, I'd like to joyfully point out, Pete even smiled. But the morning was soon ruined, like so many great times inevitably were, by parents texting and saying they'd be there in five minutes to pick me up. By the time I had grabbed my nice clothes from upstairs—Adam insisted I keep the clothes he had lent me; they smelled like him, so I wasn't about to argue—my dad had pulled into the driveway.

"I guess this is good-bye," I said, lingering at the front door.

Adam's eyes lit up, remembering something. "Wait here," he said. "I'll be right back." A moment later he returned, carrying the stained glass pendant from his bedroom. "Here. It's a little late, but Merry Christmas."

"Thanks," I said, voice catching in my throat. "I didn't get you anything."

"You already got me the best present of all," Adam began.

"Just stop right there. There's no way you could possibly end that sentence that doesn't result in me rolling my eyes and making fun of how cheesy you are for the rest of your life."

"I can think of one thing you wouldn't make fun of me for."

"Oh yeah? What's that?"

Instead of responding, Adam pulled me to him and kissed me, deeply and passionately. From the kitchen, Pete called, "Ew, gross," but Adam ignored him.

Breathless and giddy, I said, "See you Monday," and ran out to the car.

CHAPTER TWENTY-SIX

"SO, WHAT'S going to happen now?" Kai asked as we walked down the school hallway toward the lunchroom.

"I don't know. Do I look like I'm psychic?" I snapped. I could feel Kai and Mel exchange looks behind my back. I knew what they were thinking, but I wasn't being irrational. I was just on edge.

"I mean, do you want an honest answer?" Mel began, in her typical playfully mocking tone. "'Cause I *have* noticed...."

Kai cut her off. "What I meant was, haven't you two talked since yesterday?"

"I mean, we've texted, but it was mostly just, like, casual flirty stuff. Sorry I didn't immediately start demanding 'What happens on Monday when I see you? Do I have to go back to lying?' 'Cause that was a little hard to work into the conversation." A sudden thought paralyzed me. "Oh my God, what if he's been avoiding me all day? Usually we see him by now, right? What if everything is just going to be back the way it was? I don't know if I can—"

"Whoa, Dylan, breathe, dude," Kai said. "I'm sure everything will be fine. Adam's a good dude. Presumably. I'm still kind of taking that one on faith—"

"Focus, Malachi," Mel whispered.

"—but whatever, you guys seem to like him now, I'll take your word for it. I mean, he told his brother, Dylan, which is a pretty big deal. He said he loves you. It's still hard for me to imagine those words coming out of his mouth—"

"Seriously? I said focus!"

"—but that only makes it even more profound, coming from him, right? And then there's that stained glass pendant, which is apparently significant?"

Mel nodded. "Dylan did bring it up like six times."

"Right? I'm still fuzzy as to *why*."

I cut them off. Left alone they might have gone on like that forever. "Shut up, guys, It harkens back to our first night together, when I started sharing parts of myself with him."

"Stained-glass-related parts?" Kai said.

"What? There are sides of me you don't know about."

"That's exactly my point. How long have you lived this secret stained glass life? Do you have secret stained glass friends? Is there a secret stained glass Kai? Oh my God, do you like him better than me? *Are we the 'other family'?*"

"What Malachi was *trying* to say, before his neuroses got the better of him," Mel broke in, "is that Adam is *not* avoiding you, you'll go in that lunchroom, and whatever happens, we've got your back. It'll be fine."

"I bet stained glass Kai doesn't have your back," Kai muttered to himself.

In a perfect world, when I walked into that lunchroom, all eyes would have been on me. Heads would have turned, conversations immediately cut off, maybe even dramatic noontime-shootout-type music would have played. But we don't live in a perfect world, and all I got was the typical bustle of hundreds of disinterested teenagers.

In a slightly less than perfect world, this disinterested crowd would have casually parted, revealing Adam across the way, bathed in a beam of sunlight, perhaps astride a white horse. But we don't live in a slightly less than perfect world. Adam wasn't even in the lunchroom.

In a "not at all perfect but still pretty agreeable" world, Adam would have entered right then, and maybe all the above scenarios would follow smoothly from there. Instead, Mel, Kai, and I had time to wait in line, get our lunches, pay for them, sit at our table, and eat a few begrudging mouthfuls.

Then he arrived.

The entire football team entered the lunchroom in a pack, like they so often did. Adam was at the head of the group. Our eyes met. We came toward each other as though drawn by some irresistible force until we stood at the dead center of the lunchroom, surrounded by almost everyone we'd ever known. I could feel what was about to happen. I began to shake, ever so slightly, as I became terribly aware of everyone being able to see me in a way I hadn't felt in a long time. By the way his eyes darted around the room, I could tell Adam felt the same way. Is this how he always felt when we were together in public? I think I was mostly feeling it out of sympathy and expectation, but even so it was nearly overwhelming. Would he go through with it? Finally acknowledge me in front of everyone? I could see him teetering on the edge of a decision, torn between fear and determination.

Then he kissed me.

It was short, awkward, and somewhat off-putting. But all the same, it felt as though someone had lit off fireworks in the building, a choir of angels began to sing sweeping love ballads as the earth quaked and volcanoes erupted heart-shaped plumes of molten rock and clouds of ash wrote large our names across the heavens, all somehow rolled into the time it took for a single hurried peck on the lips. It was like the world stopped turning and said how about we just take a minute to savor this moment. I half expected the entire lunchroom to burst into an expertly choreographed song-and-dance number before the curtain slammed shut and the audience went home all teary eyed—after a standing ovation, maybe a few encores.

In reality, it was a two-second affair that went largely unnoticed. I mean, Will Davis's eyes were bulging nearly out of their sockets, a couple of Adam's jock buddies had quizzical looks on their faces, and someone (almost certainly Mel) whistled loudly. Everyone else in the lunchroom just went about their day. Except for Tiffany saying "Well, that makes a *lot* of things make sense." Adam's de facto coming out went entirely unremarked upon. But strangely, Adam looked unhappy.

"Are you okay?" I asked. "What is it?"

"I'm fine. It's just, you spend your whole life being afraid, like really dreading something, and then nothing happens.... I know I should be happy, but instead I'm...."

"Disappointed?" I finished for him.

"Yes!" he said. "That's exactly it. Is that weird?"

"No. I mean, yeah, kind of, but I get it. It's like, what was the big deal, then?"

"And why did I go through all that trouble to hide it if no one even cares?"

"And you want people to care."

"Or at least notice!"

"Don't worry," I said, "I got you. Oy," I called over my shoulder to Tiffany. "Bitch, you did *not* just ignore me when I'm trying to start some drama."

"Oh right," she said. "Let me try again."

Adam looked confused "What does she mean—" I interrupted him by grabbing his head with both hands and kissing him. This time, Tiffany's shrill shriek cut through the lunchroom, disrupting the casual hustle-bustle.

"Hands off my man, you slut!"

This time heads turned, and the rapid susurrus of gossip filled the air. James gave us a thumbs-up and Charlotte shook her head. We were instantly the center of attention. The only two people who weren't focused on us was that new kid and Will Davis, who appeared to be trapped in a heated discussion. But I didn't pay them any mind.

"That better?" I asked.

"I expected a bit more chaos. At least some outrage," he said.

"Wait for it...." As always, Mel was quick on the uptake. She leapt up on the table, pointing like a madwoman, and screamed, "*Death to gays!*" With her other hand, she let loose a mushed-up clump of Tater Tots, which expanded in the air to splatter across several tables.

In my experience, there are a few things high schoolers will leap at the opportunity to do. Things like gossip and finding any excuse to avoid homework, and anything that even implies sexy times. But more than anything else, the kids of Oak Lake High constantly itched for a food fight.

As our classmates, en masse, turned the lunchroom into a war zone, Adam kissed me again, this time slowly, luxuriating in the moment.

Around us, meatballs exploded against walls like fireworks, a choir of screaming girls filled the air with sweet music, and the floor shook as people dove behind tables. Heart-shaped squirts of spaghetti sauce abounded and, if I could have taken a picture at the exact right moment, I'm sure one of the many airborne tangles of noodles would have spelled our names.

"Now this is more the fanfare I expected," Adam said with a smile.

"Strangely, not too far from what I was picturing too."

PRINCIPAL HAYES regarded us over steepled fingers. "What am I going to do with you two?"

Adam and I shared a look. "Whatever do you mean?" Adam said. He was innocence incarnate.

"You incited a riot." Hayes said flatly.

I scoffed loudly. "We can hardly be held accountable for other people's actions. To imply otherwise would be a refutation of free will, to say the least."

Hayes sighed. "Am I to believe your… actions to be another misguided attempt at theater?"

"Naw," Adam said. "This was clearly an attempt at performance art."

"Adam wanted to cover himself in blood and run through the hallways naked, but I talked him out of it."

"Don't give me that look, Mr. Hayes. It would have been pig's blood."

"Right." Mr. Hayes pinched the bridge of his nose with his thumb and forefinger. "What am I going to do with you two?"

"You already said that," I remarked.

"You could give us both detention. I'm sure we'd find a way to pass the time." Adam's grin bordered on evil.

"Just get back to class," Mr. Hayes said, waving us away in defeat.

Adam put his arm around my shoulder as we walked out of Hayes's office. "It's good to be back," he said.

"Isn't it? Bye, Mr. Hayes. We'll see you tomorrow, I'm sure."

DIRK HUNTER grew up in a small farmhouse just west of Beleriand before it sank. He currently lives in Southeast Minneapolis, where he spends most of his time writing, playing video games, and desperately trying to avoid fading into the West.

DIRTY Dining
EM LYNLEY

MOMENTS IN TIME: BOOK ONE
MOMENT
OF IMPACT
KAREN STIVALI

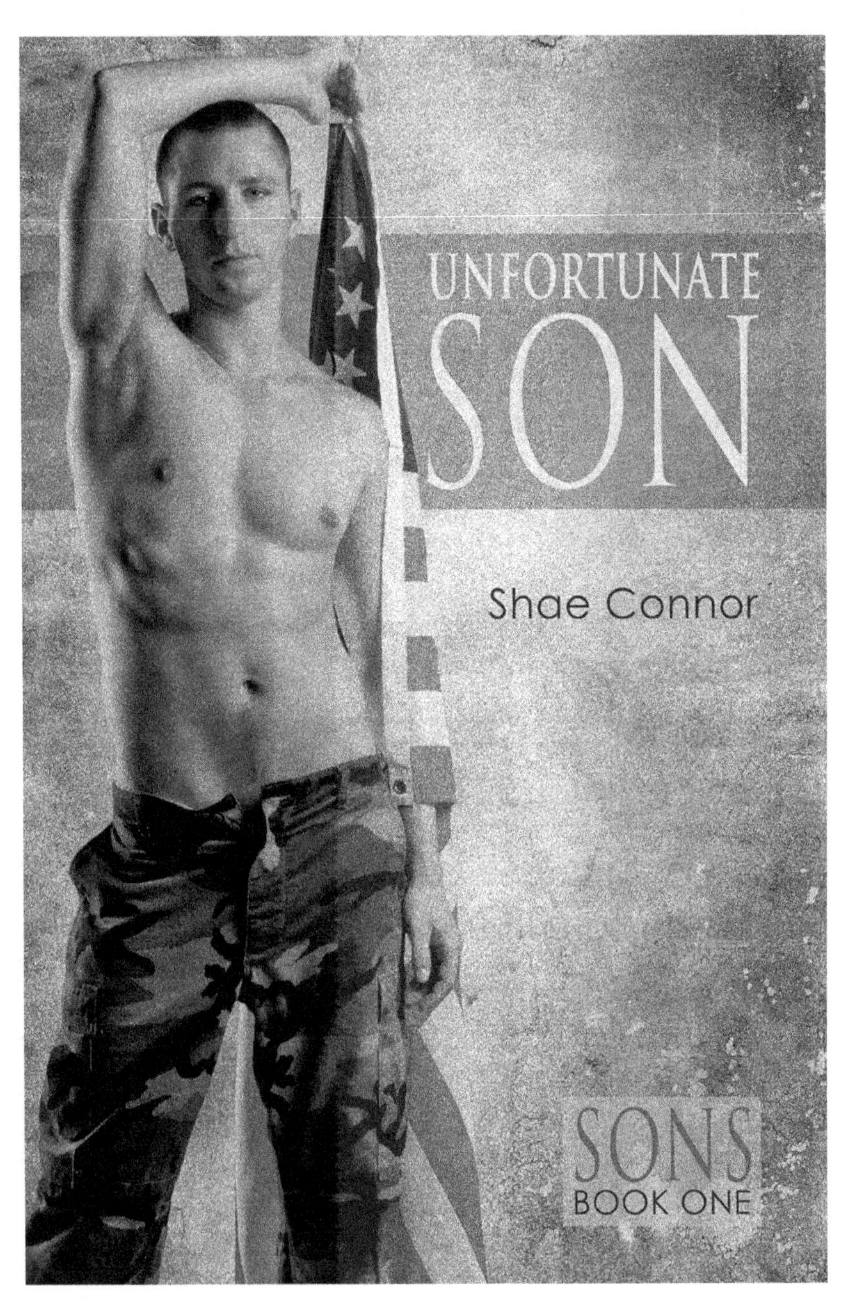

http://www.dreamspinnerpress.com

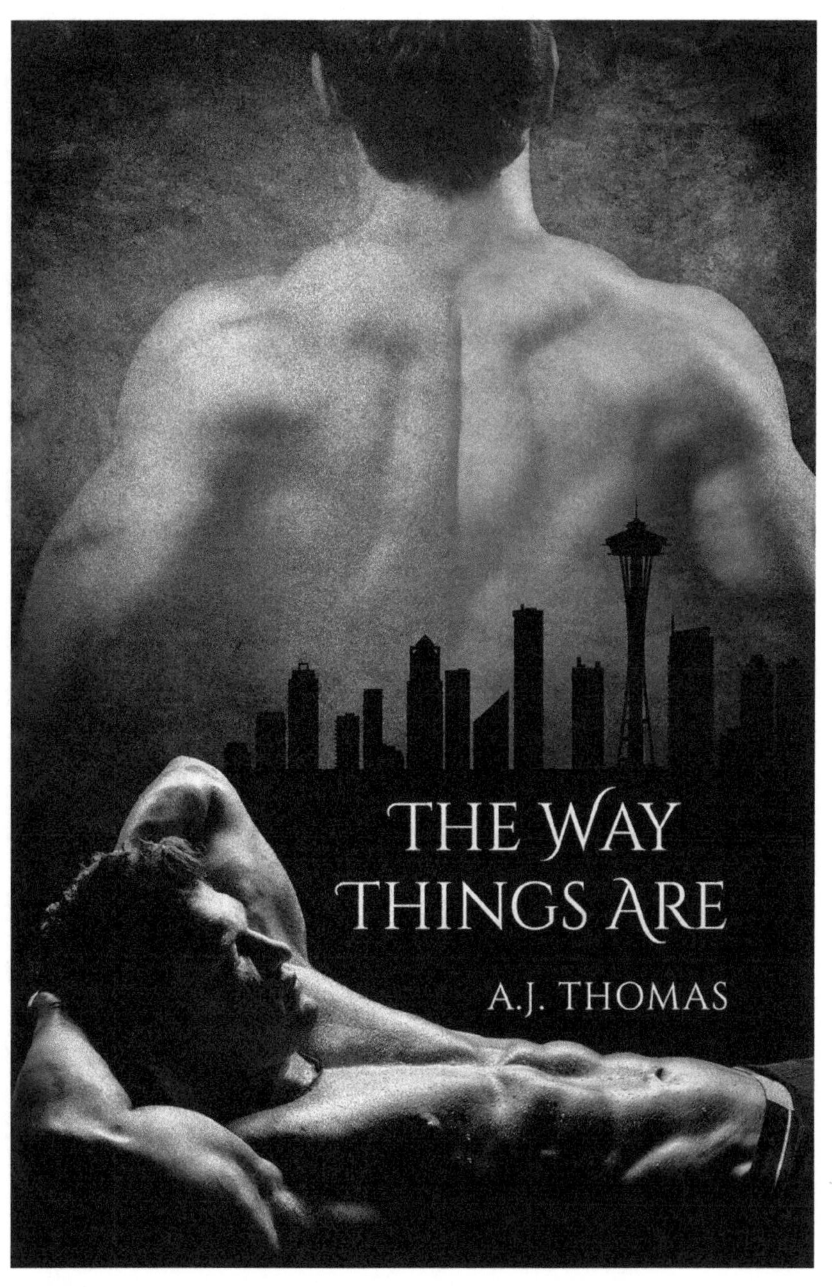
THE WAY
THINGS ARE
A.J. THOMAS

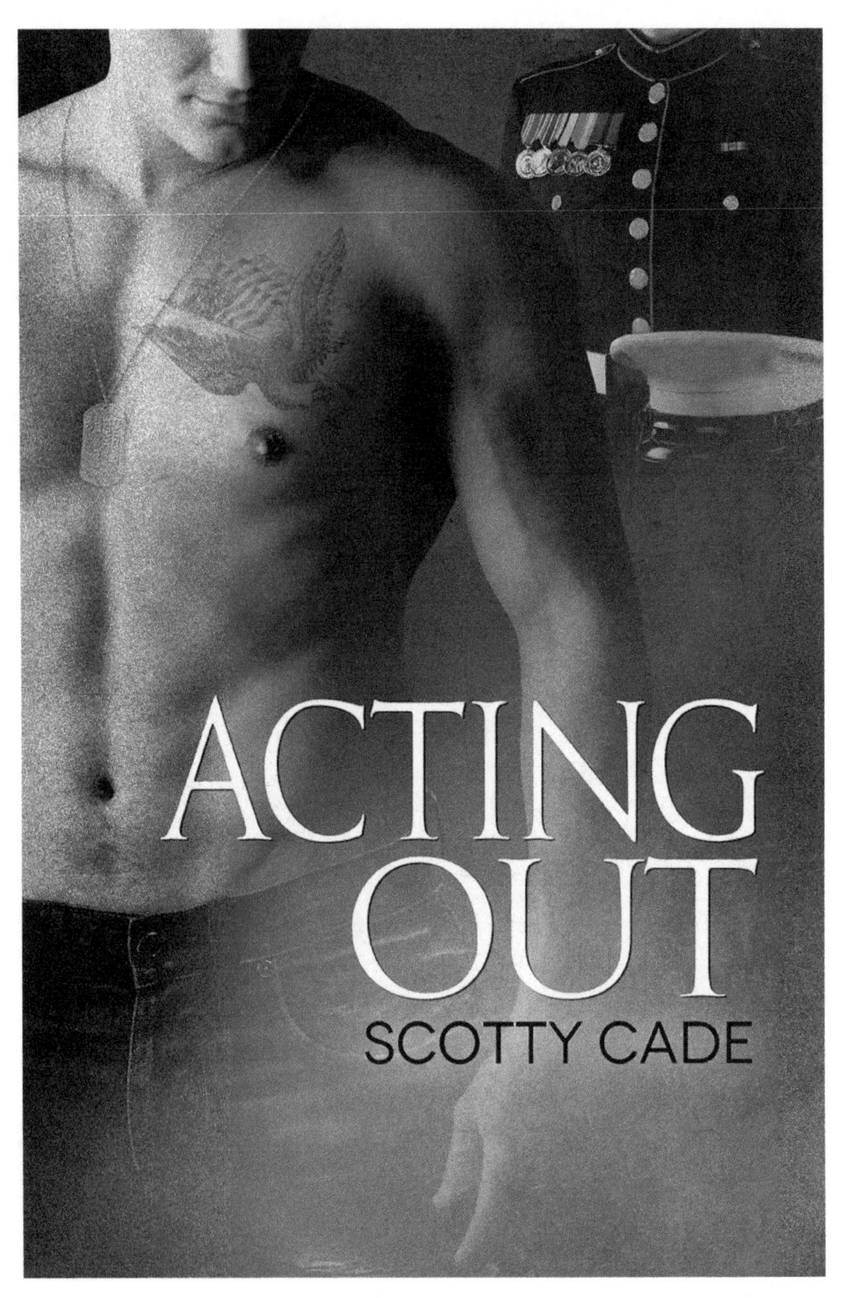

http://www.dreamspinnerpress.com

http://www.dreamspinnerpress.com

http://www.dreamspinnerpress.com

http://www.dreamspinnerpress.com

NOT JUST
FRIENDS
JAY NORTHCOTE

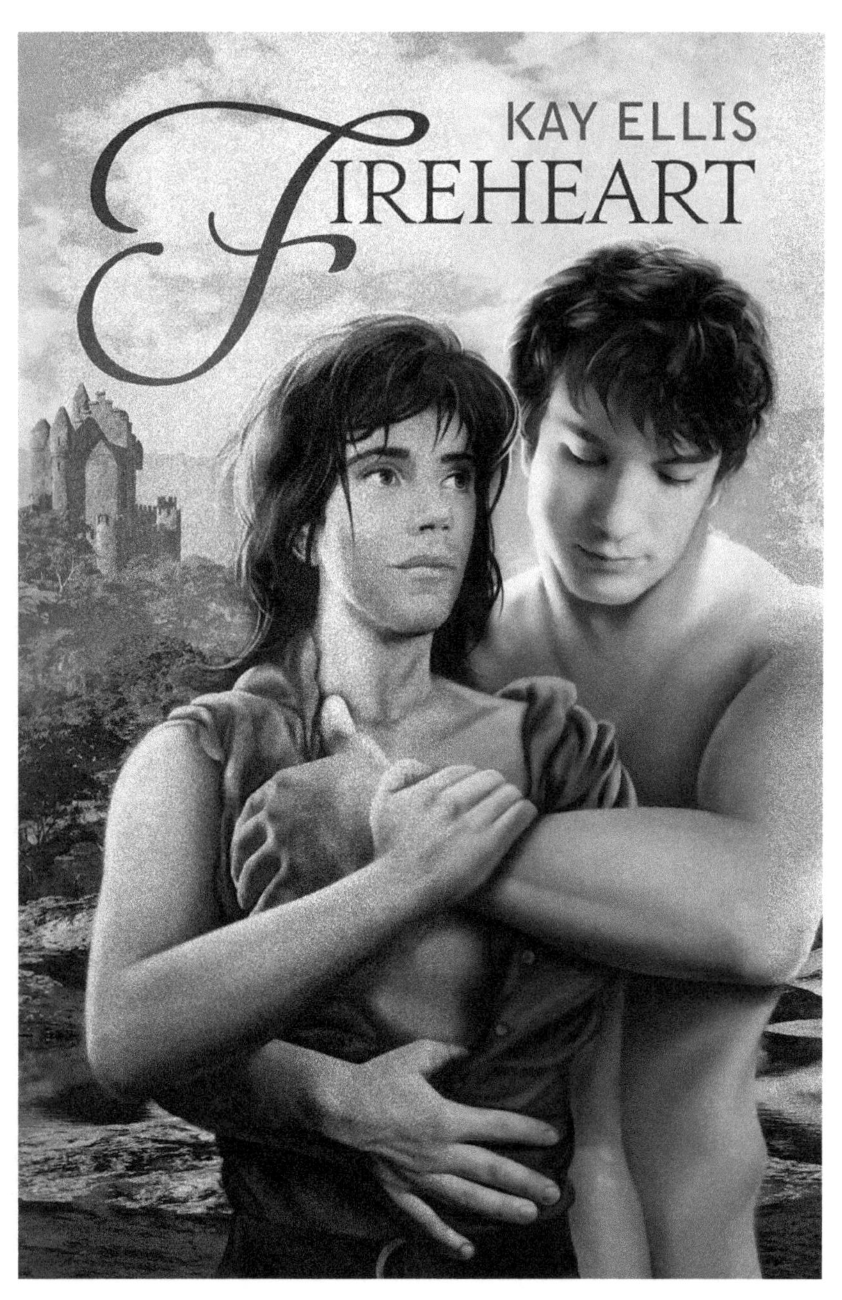
KAY ELLIS
FIREHEART

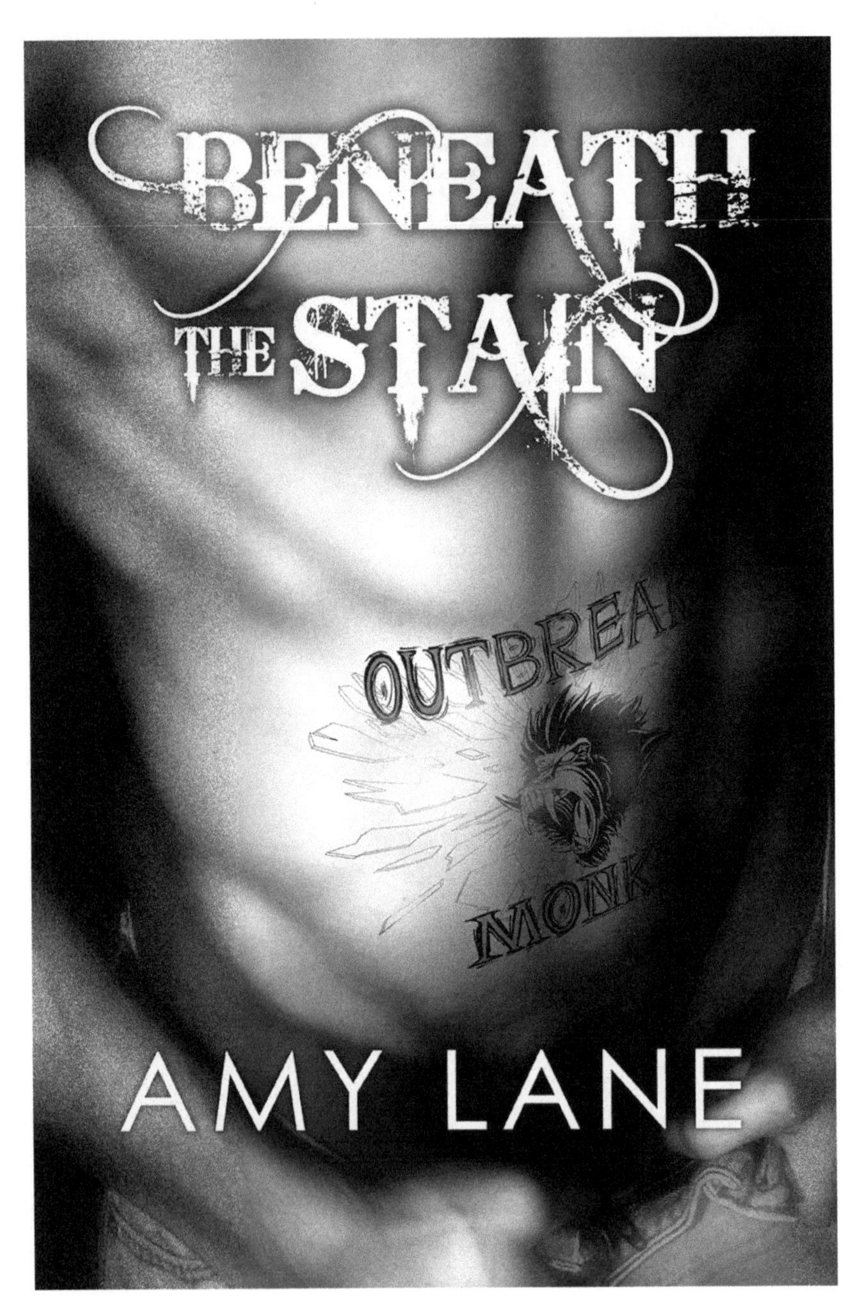

http://www.dreamspinnerpress.com

FAR
FROM HAPPY
JENI DECKER

FOR
MORE
OF THE
BEST
GAY
ROMANCE
Dreamspinner Press
DREAMSPINNERPRESS.COM